BIG BLACK DOG IN VALLARTA

BIG BLACK DOG IN VALLARTA

Mary Branham

SUNSTONE PRESS
SANTA FE

Pen and Ink cover art and chapter illustrations:
"Training the Corn Dog" © 1996 by Dennis Culver
from "Homage to Perplexiquitl".

Sunstone books may be purchased for educational, business, or sales promotional use. For information please write: Special Markets Department, Sunstone Press, P.O. Box 2321, Santa Fe, New Mexico 87504-2321.

FIRST EDITION

Library of Congress Cataloging in Publication Data:

Branham:, Mary, 1929–
Big black dog in Vallarta / Mary Branham. — 1st ed.
p. cm.
ISBN: 0-86534-277-6 (hardcover) ISBN: 978-1-63293-108-5 (softcover)
1. Dogs—Mexico—Fiction. I. Title.
PS3552. R3238B73 1998
813'.54—dc21 98-40412
CIP

Published by SUNSTONE PRESS
Post Office Box 2321
Santa Fe, NM 87504-2321 / USA
(505) 988-4418 / *orders only* (800) 243-5644
FAX (505) 988-1025

For Ernie and Kay and Lyn
who went to the party in Vallarta

Am I going to Mexico to help Maude commit suicide or to keep her from killing herself, Sydney Reardon tried to decide as she settled into an aisle seat on the Mexicana morning flight to Puerto Vallarta. She regretted the lack of a first class section but by being on the aisle her long legs managed well enough.

The flight was perfect for an afternoon arrival and she had always liked this airline. They flew anywhere one wanted to go in Mexico. The service was attentive and the food was better than on many U.S. airlines. The choice would probably be quiche or quesadillas.

But what the menu offered today was neither and was not of much interest. Since Maude's call at noon yesterday nothing had seemed important, especially food.

Sydney had been rushing out to meet the Rasmussons for lunch at the Palace to talk about the old adobe they wanted re-done when she had heard the phone ring. Where had she put it this time? Often buried under a cushion to muffle the sound.

"Hello," she said breathlessly.

There was a chuckle. "I love the way you answer the phone, sounding as if you had run to pick it up because you were rushing either in or out. I've always thought it was a ploy. In case you don't want to talk you can say you're in a hurry. You did the same thing when we were kids."

"So you've told me often. Where are you?"

"Darlin' I'm in Vallarta as I usually am this time of year. The weather is grand. Come on down."

"It's beautiful here too. It's been snowing. You know I love Santa Fe this time of year."

"This is not a casual invitation. I need you to come." Maude's voice was now serious. "Right away. Tomorrow."

"I can't get away that quickly. I'm in the midst of things."

"Sydney, I'm going to kill myself. It's all arranged. All you have to do is hold my hand so I don't lose my nerve."

"Jesus, Maude. That's not funny. I know you like bizarre humor but this is too much."

"It's not humor. Please. Come tomorrow. You promised."

"I promised?"

"We made a pact, remember. We were studying about Cleopatra and we said if either of us ever decided to end it all the other would help."

"I don't remember that at all. I'd never have agreed to such a thing."

"You did. Cross my heart and hope to die."

"If I did I didn't mean it. Anyway, that was a million years ago. We thought we were immortal. What on earth is wrong?"

"I'll tell you all. Will you be on that Mexicana flight from LA that gets in early afternoon?"

"Of course."

"We'll meet you. Oh, we'll have a party first." Maude cackled and hung up.

Sydney put the telephone down slowly and then picked it up abruptly and rang the restaurant to tell them she would be late.

She poured a strong Johnny Walker Black and sat down in front of the morning fire still glowing in the corner fireplace. She shuddered. After staring into the embers for a few minutes and sipping the Scotch, she then felt she could face a working lunch.

Yes, she would see about antique gates and doors from Mexico. She could come up with exquisite fabric woven right here in northern New Mexico. Folk art did seem a good idea for the portals. Probably Mexican but perhaps some Navajo.

Back at home after lunch she felt less disturbed by the call because there were things to be done. Pack. For a party or a funeral? Don't be fatuous, Sydney chided herself. She smiled, remembering Maude's parting words about a party. Be practical, she decided. Pack for both.

Why not go to Los Angeles to spend the night rather than get up before dawn and drive in the snow to the airport in Albuquerque.

Now, as she sipped the orange juice *especial* as they called it in

Mexico when you laced it with vodka, she replayed Maude Adams' call for the umpteenth time.

Maude was perfectly capable of putting on an act to persuade her to come for a party. If it was an act it was convincing. In school Maude could faint at will when called to the blackboard to solve a problem if she didn't know the answer. And she always stammered and called the headmaster "Daddy" when she was being reprimanded. She'd follow this slip with a tearful, "I'm sorry, you just remind me so much of my father." It worked over and over.

The first time she had seen Maude she was in tears, standing in the quadrangle trying to decide which path to follow. Sydney was dashing from swimming to change clothes for dinner but she stopped beside the forlorn girl who had obviously just arrived at midterm.

"Hi. I'm Sydney Reardon."

The big girl looked at her with bright, tear-filled eyes and smiled self-consciously revealing a row of metal on her upper teeth. "I'm Maude Adams. I'm lost."

"Were you named for the actress?"

"I don't know who that is. Our family name is Adams and my grandmother's name was Maude."

Later, when she married Robert Crenfell she kept the Adams and just added Crenfell with a hyphen. Bob wanted her to keep Adams, she said. Rob and Lucy were always Crenfell but that was simpler for children. Maude had friends and acquaintances all over the globe and probably about half thought of her as Adams and the rest as Crenfell. Sydney couldn't think of anyone except bankers and service people who used the two names. She was probably listed that way on credit cards. Everyone in the Vallarta household referred to her as Señora Maude.

But she'd always been plain Maude Adams to Sydney.

"No matter how you were named," Sydney said that blustery winter afternoon. "Come on. I'll show you the way."

She smiled over her breakfast remembering the braces, the shiny eyes and the unbelievable accent.

They had been friends ever since.

The three women sipping margaritas beside the river at Le Bistro had one thing in common. They were close friends of Maude's. Actually, they shared an additional interest. They loved the west coast of Mexico.

Julia Lundgren was the oldest by far. She had migrated to Vallarta on each Monday after Thanksgiving since 1975 and returned to Chicago the second Monday in March. For all those years she had enjoyed the same fifth floor room at the Camino Real, gazing morning and evening out across Banderas Bay and, in her mind's eye, across the Pacific.

On odd-numbered years her children, grandchildren, and now great-grandchildren, spent Christmas week with her at the hotel. Other years the family went about their own lives and she invited friends to join her for the holidays to relax on the white sand of Playa las Estacas. Next month she would be eighty and she thought of no reason to change her routine.

When Maude began coming to Vallarta, Chicago friends insisted that she look up Julia Lundgren. They had clicked at once.

Valenciana Tello owned a smart shop on a narrow street a block back from the *malecón* toward the hills. She also owned a shop in the Zona Rosa in Mexico City and it was there she spent most of the year. However, from the first of December to the first of March she left the shop just off the Reforma in the hands of her husband while she enjoyed the balmy tropical weather of Vallarta and the influx of visitors from north of the border.

She didn't really like tourists from the United States much and she was pleased when she could take advantage of them on a sale. But she liked Maude and she was pretty certain she couldn't take advantage of her even if she tried.

Valenciana's father had labored as a boy in a small mine in Guanajuato as a *caballito*—little horse, as those carrying ore out of the mines on their backs were called. Years later, when he was a waiter in Mexico City, he had named his first-born after that grandest of all mines in his native state.

He had been dead almost a year when Maude and Valenciana met at a gallery opening and Maude's greeting was, "Darlin' black is so becoming you should stay in mourning forever."

Edwina Mead was an enigma. She and her husband had bought a house in Gringo Gulch not too long after Burton and Taylor were cavorting on the hillside above the town and it had become fashionable. They never spent more than a month or so a year there—Phillip fishing and Edwina playing bridge—and she said she didn't like the town at all.

It was curious that after Phillip died four years ago Edwina continued to spend Decembers in PV, as she called it.

Just after sunup Maude was walking on the beach when she was accosted by an enormous brindle Great Dane. Or, more correctly, she was nuzzled and licked. Looking up and down the stretch of sand for its owners she saw no one. She placed her hands firmly on the neck of the animal and inspected the tag.

"Come along," Maude said in a friendly way and Baby—according to the name on the collar—trotted after her. Telephone service being what it is in Vallarta, it was late afternoon before Edwina Mead arrived to claim Baby. By then the big dog was sunning herself on the patio after a refreshing dip in the pool. Maude was enjoying a martini in the shade nearby.

"Do join me."

Before Edwina left they had agreed that they both loved dogs more than most humans. It was the beginning of a fast friendship.

Suddenly, there was a booming laugh at the restaurant entrance.

"There's our Maude," Valenciana said.

The trio looked expectantly toward the door as Maude moved across the tile floor and out onto the deck and embraced each of them. "Sorry I'm a mite late. Sydney's arriving this afternoon and I've been busier than a one-armed paper-hanger getting ready."

She removed her black linen jacket and straightened the bosom of her black and white polka dot dress. Maude Adams was prominent in Vallarta for a number of reasons: her philanthropy, her parties, her raucous laugh, and especially because she always wore black in a resort peopled mostly by white- and pastel-clad natives and visitors.

As she eased down in her favorite chair a martini appeared. "Thank you Adrian. Are you ready for another?" She waved a hand across the table toward the almost empty margarita glasses. "Adrian, bring a pitcher. We're starting the party. Sydney loves to party and we're beginning right now. Have you met Sydney? I don't think so. She's been here often but always in and out. Even when we were building my house she was here just a couple of days at a time.

"She scolds me when I say she was responsible for the house. But she really was. When she said we should create a gem of a colonial replica I remarked that there were not many of that sort along the water. We go in more for glass and beach-front glitz and she asked, 'Do you want your house to look like every other place on the beach?' Of course not.

"And when she suggested ochre for the exterior I asked what color is that? She really prefers places like Oaxaca with all those soft-toned houses and folk art and those ruins. But, of course, she met John in Oaxaca so it will always be special."

Maude looked at her companions anticipating an answer to her first question which had been have you met Sydney.

The women who shared her table were accustomed to Maude's incessant flow of words and to the fact that she always answered her own questions while going right on with an endless monologue.

"No," Edwina said. "I haven't met her. She's a longtime friend I know."

Valenciana shook her head. "I'm surprised that I haven't. You mention her often and I remember that she's responsible for your fabulous house."

"I know her." Julia Lundgren smiled. "She's a delight."

"Since school days," Maude went on, following up on Edwina's comment. "My folks struck oil and all of a sudden we had oodles of money and Ma decided I should get a polish." Maude threw back her head and laughed. "God knows I needed a polish. I was running to fat even then and the first thing they'd done when we got rich was put braces on my teeth. I was a sad-looking case when they sent me off to this fancy school. I got there in the middle of the year so I didn't know anyone.

"I couldn't even find the dining room. I was standing in the middle of this great big yard surrounded by brick buildings with lots of white woodwork and long porches and I started to cry. This gorgeous creature came along and said, 'Hi. Are you lost?'

"Yeah," I slobbered. She smiled a brilliant smile and led me to the dining room. She was tall already and slim, slim and I thought she was wonderful. I've thought so ever since.

"We've been through a lot. Three husbands for her and my crazy divorce from Bob. Did I ever tell you about how all her husbands died and how superstitious she is?"

Before her friends could answer Maude was off and running.

"When she was eleven or twelve her mother took her to a fortune teller and the woman said she'd outlive her husbands. Later, I think when she was in college, she went to a fortune teller again. Don't ask me why. This one told her she'd have three husbands and outlive them all.

"Well, Darlin's, she has. The first one was a cute boy about her own age. He got his head blown off in Vietnam and she got his insurance money.

"The next one was a lot older. Elliott Townsend, a big-time theater producer. She was an actress then. He died of a heart attack. She felt like she didn't want to stay on in the theater after Townie died. She said she was too old to be an ingenue and not talented enough to be a leading lady. That's when she turned to decorating. He left her plenty but I suppose he was wise when he set it up so she's on some kind of allowance.

"John, the last one, was an archaeologist, or an anthropologist. I never can remember the difference. She met him in a bar in Oaxaca. He was a love. I think maybe the love of her life. They were here together for a few days once. Damned if he didn't step off a curb in little old Santa Fe and get killed by a woman on the way to church with her tiny daughters. He didn't have a whole lot to leave except a great two-hundred-year-old mud house in the right part of town."

"You talk about money from husbands. From the fancy school and her way of life I should have guessed there was family money. I remember you told us once she has had a flat in London for years." Edwina could always cut through Maude's verbal hurricane to make a point.

"They had money. Not a whole lot but long on background and real class. They're all doctors and lawyers and professors. I don't think they were too excited about her being an actress. No matter how much money Sydney had she could spend it. When times are lean she still spends. Her motto is, 'A dollar saved is a dollar wasted.' She even made payments on an emerald ring or a diamond watch when she was on thin ice.

"We'd better order. I've got to go along to the airport shortly."

Maude beckoned lightly for Adrian, menus, and another martini.

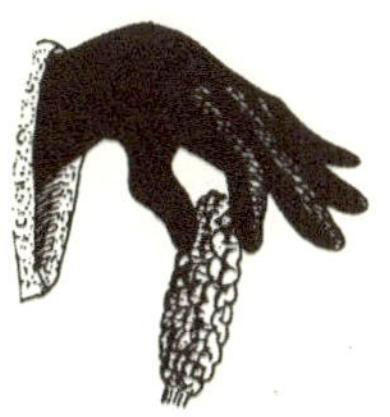

Sydney had always liked the small Mexican airports where you simply seemed to emerge from the plane and be in the middle of town. The balmy ocean air felt wonderful.

"Welcome Señora Sydney," Alfonso greeted her. "Please give me checks for your bags. Señora Maude is waiting in the car."

"I'm so glad to see you Alfonso." She took his outstretched hand in both of hers. "You look wonderful."

"You look wonderful also," he replied in his careful English and then dropped his head and smiled shyly, thinking he might have been too forward.

It pleased Sydney to see Alfonso wearing a coat and tie in this tropical resort where sneakers, jeans, shorts and sandals were pretty much the daily uniform. The luggage was now beginning to arrive and be claimed by eager passengers. As Maude's driver waited she pushed through the crowd toward the exit.

Maude was people watching, leaning casually against the front of a beautiful, shiny, old, black Cadillac convertible, and had not yet noticed her. When she hadn't seen Maude for a while Sydney was always startled by her vivacity, her energy, even in repose. She had a large head and lots of curly pale brown hair, bright eyes and big white straight teeth thanks to the braces that had earned her the nickname "Metal Mouth" at school. She was not actually much overweight but she had an ample bosom and broad shoulders, the epitome of what was often described as being larger than life.

Sydney shivered. How could anyone so vibrant be planning to end her life? It had to be a wily ruse to get her here for the party.

"Maude!"

They embraced for a long moment and then Maude stepped back and held her friend's hands.

"Darlin' I'm so glad you're here." She smiled through eyes brimming with tears.

Now Sydney knew for certain that she had not been lured to Vallarta just for this party. Her voice shook a little as she responded, "I'm glad too."

At that moment Alfonso arrived with the bags.

"Maude you have a new car," Sydney observed admiringly as Alfonso opened the trunk to stow her luggage. "It's gorgeous."

"Isn't it! It's a 1959 Eldorado Biarritz. It took a while to find just what I wanted, fully restored." She passed a hand, ornamented by two large diamonds in ornate settings, affectionately over the dark mirror-like surface. "Get in. Rides as good as it looks."

As they sank onto the black leather seats Alfonso appeared with refreshments. "Black Label." He smiled as he handed Sydney a frosted glass. "Easy on the water."

"Thank you Alfonso. You always remember." It was amusing that when Maude hired anyone she sent them to learn English so in all her years in Vallarta it had never been necessary for her to learn Spanish. Early on Sydney had used her fair Spanish to converse with Alfonso. Over time he had become proficient in English and she had noticed on recent visits that if she spoke to him in Spanish he usually answered in English.

"He remembers, and so do I, that you'd much rather have Scotch than margaritas. Most everybody drinks them but I think it is more custom than enjoyment. I still prefer martinis. Up. *Salud.*" She raised her glass.

"*Salud.*" Sydney smiled. "That's the only word I ever hear you speak in Spanish."

"Only one I know Darlin'. Only one I need."

"Maude, what's going on?" Sydney asked as Alfonso eased the long car out of airport traffic.

"I'm planning a party you'll remember forever. There are lots of entertaining new folks in town and there are loads of my friends you haven't met yet. The ones you know will be thrilled to see you. It'll be a costume party."

"A costume party?"

"I know what you're thinking. How would anyone want to come as Queen Elizabeth I or Bonaparte or Pancho Villa on a warm evening with this humidity. So it's just masks and from the neck down you wear anything you like. Or nothing." Maude roared. "I've got a great mask for you."

"Maude. . . ."

Ignoring the interruption Maude continued, "And the party will be in this divine restaurant. We're going there after a bit for drinks so you can see it and meet Hale Howard. You know he's my lawyer. You need to get acquainted. You're going to have to work together."

"Maude, what is happening? Stop the chit-chat and tell me." Sydney paused. "Sorry luv. Perhaps I shouldn't be discussing this now."

"Oh, you mean in front of Alfonso? He knows. He's the only one who does except for Hale. And, of course, the doctor. All right. I'll explain, but then you have to put it all out of your mind until after the party."

Sydney had no time to protest as Maude continued.

"The ticker is shot. Too many years of good sex and drinking and dancing, I expect.

"They say—they being the best doctors money can buy anywhere in the world—that only a heart transplant can fix me and, of course, that isn't a cinch. I just might consider it but my chances of getting a new heart are slim. Did you know there are close to fifty thousand people in the United States alone waiting for transplants? And there are maybe five thousand donors a year. You know I love to gamble but I can figure those odds. And, guess what, I'm too old to be high on the list."

"Jesus luv, you're not fifty."

Maude laughed a little shakily. "That stops you in your sneakers doesn't it. And this will get your attention. They're doing serious research to see if you can use pig hearts for transplants to humans. Some doctor who's working on that heard about me and must have heard I had lots of dollars and he made a pretty persuasive case for my giving them money for research. He even hinted I might be one of the first recipients of a pig heart."

Maude howled. "I bet there are plenty of people who'd think that was appropriate. Anyhow, I gave them a hundred thou for research and said no thanks."

"Think about it Maude. If there's no hope otherwise. Lots of people live perfectly satisfactory lives with replacement parts."

"No, Darlin', in my view, they don't. They're just willing to settle for a vastly altered lifestyle to go on and I'm not."

"When Maude? You've asked me to stand by. At least tell me when."

"No. I've thought long and hard about that. I'm convinced if I tell you it will be even more difficult because you will be counting days. And then hours. You can't help yourself. I know. I'm counting. Hale and Alfonso don't know either. No. You'll have to wait. But not for long." She nodded her head with finality.

Sydney knew Maude, and knew this conversation was finished.

"We're crossing the river. Now I feel we're really in your neighborhood. There's the house. It is so beautiful. It always gives me a thrill to see it."

"It should thrill you. You created a perfect colonial house here beside the Rio Cuale. It might seem more at home in some other setting but then I wouldn't have the Pacific Ocean in my front yard."

Alfonso had eased the elegant car carefully over the uneven cobblestones and come to a halt in front of the massive door in the garden wall, framed with grey cut stones and topped by a graceful stucco shell.

Sydney stepped out the moment he opened the door. "I can hardly wait to see the garden. You said you've done new things."

"Wait," Maude said as Alfonso helped her out. "Let me go in ahead of you."

Pretty Eloisa opened the door so quickly that she must have been waiting just inside the courtyard for the sound of the Cadillac.

The largest Chow Chow Sydney had ever seen bounded forward.

"Stay," Maude ordered as she swept her hand toward the dog's muzzle.

He stopped a foot in front of Sydney and sat smiling and wagging his entire body.

Sydney dropped to one knee. "You're so pretty." She eased a hand toward him, palm up, and the blue-black tongue reached out to welcome her. "But you're so big."

"I'm glad he likes you. I want you to take him."

"Maude, I don't want a dog."

"Of course you want a dog. Everyone wants a dog. They just don't always know it. You'll see."

"I'm away too much. It isn't fair."

"That's what people say when they haven't had a dog in a while. You've always loved my dogs. You grew up with dogs. It's time you have one again."

"I do love dogs but all those years in Manhattan I didn't have one. In London where I was right by the Green Park would have been ideal but I was away for months at a time. Santa Fe would be perfect but I don't think so—not yet. If I wanted a dog I'd be tempted. What's his name?"

"He's the Corn Dog. I call him Corn for short. Remember once when I was in Santa Fe you took me to that wonderful Munson Gallery on Canyon Road and there was a show by a writer and an artist both named Dennis. They had constructed a mythology based on a concocted god called Perplexiquitl. The inhabitants of their ancient legendary village had unlikely names like Talks to Trees, Forgets His Own Name, Feets Too Big."

"You bought one of the pen-and-ink drawings didn't you?"

"Training the Corn Dog. I was torn between that and Walking the Ur Gator. The text said many people think walking an Ur Gator is similar to walking a modern alligator. That can be a fatal mistake. According to the collaborators, many armsherds and legsherds display the unmistakable signature of the Ur Gator.

"Finally I opted for Training the Corn Dog. When I asked why the Corn Maiden had a black hand they told me it wasn't a hand, it was a glove. You should never try to train the Corn Dog without wearing a glove. I asked how you train the Corn Dog. The Dennis who is the artist said, 'Carefully.' Look, here's the drawing. I have it hanging on the portal."

"I remember. It is so amusing. And the intricacy of the work. How long have you had Corn?"

"About ten months."

"How did you get him? Knowing you, there will be a story behind it, or you've fabricated one."

"Indeed there is a story. Every word true," Maude grinned gleefully. "It's a long one. Let's sit here in the shade. Eloisa will bring some iced tea."

Sydney turned. "*Eloisa, buenas tardes.* I was so surprised by this wonderful dog that I didn't greet you properly. I'm happy to see you."

"And I to see you Señora." She disappeared to get the tea.

"An American couple abandoned the dog." Maude motioned toward a comfortable leather *equipal* chair. "I don't know how they got out of the country without him. You know the Mexican authorities at the border carry on if you bring an animal in and don't take it out. I had a friend who came for the winter and brought his Airedale. The dog died and he had one hell of a time getting back across the border without it even though he had all sorts of papers from a vet.

"Don't worry about taking Corn out of the country. All papers are in order. You brought him when you were here last February and then had to rush home and left him with me."

"In February I was in Tubac having problems with window coverings for the spa in the Overholt house. I seem to be always having curtain frustrations. I wasn't here and you know it."

"Oh yes you were," Maude stated with alacrity. "You stayed one night at the Camino Real. Intended to stay longer but were called back because of a problem at that Tubac house. I can prove you stayed at the Camino Real. For heaven's sake, no one's going to check on a dog but the hotel records prove you were here just in case they question you."

"Maude you have a devious mind. You should have been a criminal," Sydney teased.

"How do you know I'm not?"

"I've known you too long. But maybe there's room for doubt. I remember your Uncle Hobson had taught you to pick locks and you could get in and steal a quiz if we hadn't studied."

"Good old Uncle Hobson. He was the only one in our family who had any money until we struck oil. See, there was a burglar in my family. I could easily be a criminal."

"We may not have been too honest but we were certainly *naïve*."

"Anyhow, this poor animal was just running around town. The police were afraid of him because he was big and black and had that wonderful black tongue. Matter of fact, everyone was afraid because they thought he was somehow sinister.

"I heard about him and Alfonso and I went looking. We found him huddled on the steps beside the church. He was hungry and thirsty and scared. I finally lured him into the car with a chunk of meat. We put a lead on him and he had a fit and tried to jump through a window.

"Alfonso and I couldn't get him out of the car so we called Miguel. I don't think you know him. He's new to the house but you remember his mother Maria."

"Of course. The last time I was here she was complaining of arthritis in her knees."

"Right. She hasn't been able to work in a good while. After she was too crippled her daughter Della filled in but she fell and broke her ankle and it never has worked right. Miguel had been in the army and when he came home Maria asked me to give him a job. He's wiry and young and strong and does all kinds of chores and errands. And it helps Maria. We thought Miguel could pull the dog through the door into the patio. He was afraid and the dog sensed it and bared his teeth and growled and Miguel ran.

"Finally Alfonso drove as close as he could to the patio entrance and both of us held onto the lead and he dragged us inside and we slammed the door. When we took off the lead he jumped into the pool and drank and drank and swam and got out and shook water over everything and jumped in the flower beds and trampled them and then fell asleep on the orchids."

Sydney was overcome with laughter. "I don't believe it," she gasped at last.

"It's so good to hear you laugh. I don't hear that wonderful sound often enough."

"Jesus luv, if I were the same old jolly girl I once was wouldn't you think I'm some kind of nut after all that has happened?"

"Well maybe," Maude conceded going back to her story. "So help me, it's exactly what happened. Of course we couldn't let him into the house and we were afraid he'd get out if we opened the door onto the street. Miguel was terrified that I'd make him walk the dog and he didn't come back to work for a week. Eloisa spent all the day with her nose pressed against the window watching and trying to talk to him.

"I'd go out onto the patio and sit on the chaise and he'd jump across my lap and then on top of the table and look down at me wagging his tail.

"Panchita was the only one he didn't intimidate. The first night she cooked a steak for him and brought it out and I thought he'd break the plate and take her hand off. She stood her ground, all five feet of her, and spoke to him in Spanish. I don't think he understood Spanish but he sure as hell knew who was in charge. He stood still and looked at her tentatively and let her put the plate down and wagged his tail and devoured the whole thing in about three bites."

Sydney was still laughing. "I know you exaggerate but I wish I had seen it all. How is Panchita?"

"Fine. She's eager to see you. She knows you love breakfast in bed. Late. You can look forward to her wonderful scrambled eggs and chile with a brioche and your orange juice *especial*. She's still the best cook in town."

"The dog is so well trained now. How did you get him to behave?"

"After three or four days the garden was completely destroyed and my nerves were shot. I was tempted to open the door and let him run.

"Then I thought of Carlotta. You remember Carlotta Rogers who has trained several dogs for me. She shaped up that beautiful but dumb Setter I had in New Orleans. I called and asked her to come down and do something about this big black beast before he killed someone or someone killed him. The woman washing windows heard me say that and the rumor started that he was a killer. Lots of the locals are superstitious about black dogs. They're supposed to belong to witches. A black dog with a black tongue was really beyond the pale.

"Luckily Carlotta came right away. She took one look at him and what he'd done to the garden and the furniture and knew she had her work cut out. I commented that he was so big I thought he might be part Akita. She shook her head and said, 'No, he's just not a very good Chow Chow. His legs are too long; his head is too big; his coat isn't great.'" Maude guffawed. "Carlotta never was long on small talk. She always has called a spade a shovel. In spite of all those defects, isn't he handsome?"

Sydney could only nod before Maude continued.

"Carlotta thought it would take her two or three weeks to get him bathed and brushed and under control. It took six weeks but when she was leaving she told me, 'He's so lovable. Even when he's bad he's cute.' You'll see she's right. You'll love him."

"Jesus, Maude," Sydney started to protest.

Maude interrupted, as always. "After he was shaped up I had to start over with the garden and I had this wonderful idea about petunias. I have a friend who has a spectacular house on the cliffs above the bay down south. She has thousands of petunias. I thought to hell with exotics, let's plant more petunias than there are in the whole town. It turns out Corn doesn't care for petunias so he never goes near them."

"They are unbelievable. I couldn't picture it when you told me what you'd done. You said they make a statement. And they do! Marvelous."

Maude beamed with satisfaction. "Now you go. You're going to stay in my room."

"Oh Maude, I can't."

"Of course you can. You'll love it. You'll love the view and sitting out on the portal above the bay. Before you protest, it's not that I'm so sweet. It's that I can't always climb the stairs and I've been sleeping downstairs a lot. Sometimes I'm fine, like today, and sometimes I have to sit down and rest every few steps. Tell Eloisa what you need and she'll unpack for you. We're meeting Hale at Café des Artistes for drinks. It will be between lunch and dinner so it will be quiet and I can show you what I've planned. I want you to see the restaurant. It's such a happy place for a party.

"And, as I told you, I want you and Hale to get to know one another. It's going to be a difficult time and I'm counting on you to stand by him. His first hurdle will be reading the will to the children and I've told him you'll be there.

"Rob will be angry and petulant and make no effort to mask his feelings. He's dependent upon me. Whether he knows it or not, he's never imagined the world without Ma in it.

"Lucy will probably be ecstatic over the thought of money. But she may fall apart."

"I'll do whatever I can. You know that."

"Yes, I do." She smiled wistfully and patted Sydney's hand. "Go along. I'll be up in a few minutes to show you your mask."

"I could spend hours on your upper portal looking out at the bay."

"I do," Maude said as she sat beside Sydney among soft off-white cushions on the wicker couch. "In the morning I watch the fishing boats go out. The snorkeling ones headed for Los Arcos. The catamarans plopping along. The tourist ferries going to Yelapa. In the early evening the booze cruise goes out with music blaring.

"I look at all the boatloads of tourists and wonder about them. There are flocks who come to get toasted. They're seriously into sun and sand and skin cancer. And there are those who think it's romantic to have sex on the beach by moonlight. And you can count on those who hope to break the record for the number of margaritas they can consume."

Sydney laughed softly and placed her arm lightly across her friend's shoulders. "Maude you sound jaded about tourists. You complain just as it's popular to do in Santa Fe. We're so dependent upon tourism and yet most everyone tries to avoid downtown in summer and you hear unimaginative tourist jokes at every cocktail party. It's the same in Rome and the Hamptons and on Mykonos I dare say. I love being a tourist here."

"It is a great town for just relaxing. It's not like Paris where you have to do the Louvre. Or London where there's all that theater. Or, for that matter, Mexico City, with the special anthropology museum and the pyramids."

"John and I had a great time."

"I'm sorry your stay was so short. Did you lie in the sun or have sex on the beach or drink margaritas?"

Sydney nodded and grinned. "Probably all of the above and lots of other touristy things. Shopping. And, even a house tour. John took a parasail ride. You can be sure with my fear of heights I stayed on the ground. When were we here?" She sighed. "Two years ago."

"Oh my god Darlin'. Don't tell me you're going to ruin my party by talking about that marvelous man."

"I promise I won't. I will think about him though." She sighed again and, changing the subject, pointed to the bay. "I notice that the cruise ships get taller and fatter and whiter every time I'm here."

"And more of them. When I first started coming here there was one every week or ten days. Now, some mornings I look out and there are two or three in the bay."

"The other Sunday in the travel section I read that Banderas Bay is the largest natural bay in Mexico. I know it is huge but I never thought about it being the largest. A hundred miles of shore line."

"You always have been great at remembering unimportant information like that," Maude teased.

"I know. I sometimes have trouble with pertinent statistics but I'm remarkable at trivia."

"Speaking of statistics, I've decided I'm a classic. I have 2.5 children. Rob is such an overachiever he's probably a hundred sixty-five percent, and Lucy doesn't give a damn and is about eighty-five percent. Add them together and I have the 2.5 children you always read about."

"Maude you're terrible. How is Lucy? Where is she now?"

"She's fine so far as she's concerned. It's iffy from my viewpoint. She's tending bar in a chic little place in Palm Beach and living on a houseboat with a computer type. She's so beautiful. Why couldn't she have been a model or something instead of a peripatetic bartender? She's such fun. But she is exhausting. I can't be around her too long at a time. She works hard and they love her everywhere but you know three or four months is a career for her."

"She was wonderful trying to help me recover when I was here that Christmas after Townie died. You wanted to keep me busy and you would send Lucy out with me every day. We would walk along the *malecón* and eat ice cream cones in the morning and talk about life. When we'd walked enough we'd sit on one of those uncomfortable iron benches by the water and watch the local children playing and tourists in wrinkled khaki shorts and fanny packs all wearing clean new tee-shirts they'd just bought. Lucy had lots of fun flirting with the tourist police decked out in their white shirts and shorts and socks and their polished black shoes. They adored having her ask questions.

"We would have lunch in some fun place and in the afternoon drink beer waiting for siesta to be over so we could go shopping. She was in love with a dashing *older* man. As I remember he was almost thirty. He was going to teach her to be a bookie."

"Oh my god! I'd forgotten all about Steve. He lasted almost six months. The next one had another get-rich-quick scheme. It's ironic, she always talks about lots of money and I probably haven't been as generous as I should have. Certainly not as generous as I could have been. I thought she'd just blow it. Now she's going to have twelve million dollars. I was planning to set up a trust fund but Hale persuaded me that wasn't fair. When I told him she'll run right through it he said, 'Let her. That won't be your responsibility.' Unusual advice for a lawyer but Hale is an unusual guy. You'll see. On the other hand Rob will invest his wisely and never spend any capital."

"Is Rob's divorce final?"

"Just a few weeks ago. He and Kevin are living with what Rob calls his significant other, wherever the hell that term comes from. She's beautiful but serious and driven like Rob so they'll probably live happily ever after. She has two little girls and they seem to like Rob and get along with Kevin and vice versa."

"Kevin was almost the most beautiful baby I've ever seen. His mother was stunning."

"Oh yes. Kera was gorgeous. Still is. She's kind of a flake but I love her. Why Rob thought they could make a go of it is beyond me. To Kera life is a lark. I adore my son but he is totally humorless and excessively ambitious. And overly structured."

"I remember Kera as a sheer delight."

"I'm leaving her some money with instructions to spend it frivolously," Maude chuckled. "As if she needed to be told that."

"That's very generous."

"I know. As they say, you can't take it with you. I worry a little about Kevin. Sometimes I wish he were more like his mother. He's structured and competitive just like his father. Can you believe at eight he's the golf champion in his age group at the country club."

Sydney smiled as she knew was expected.

"Rob doesn't like Vallarta because there are no memorable ruins or famous museums or ornate churches. Even on vacation he needs to be doing something worthwhile.

"He calls this place Ma's Madhouse. But he does concede that you made a faithful copy of a colonial beauty. I've heard him telling friends that everything you did was totally in character. I see him standing down on the beach looking back at the graceful double arches and the wonderful stonework around the entrance. He's fascinated by the constantly changing patterns made by light and shadows."

"I'm flattered that he approves."

"Of course he thinks it is too grand for the neighborhood and says it can never be sold for what it's worth. I tell him he doesn't need to worry about selling it—I'll give it away. He cringes at that. He just doesn't know how soon."

Maude paused for breath and a silence fell between them. Then she was reaching to the table behind the lounge where they were sitting.

"Look! Your mask."

"She's not pretty," Sydney observed as she took the face Maude was holding. "But she looks strong. And interesting. Who is she?"

"You're absolutely right. She is strong. She's popular. All the Mexicans at the party will recognize her. She's the Corregidora."

"She was a hero person of John's. He was intrigued by her sitting in an upstairs parlor in her beautiful house in Queretaro, allegedly reading poetry but actually plotting an uprising with all those revolutionary types."

"Right. Doña Josefa Ortiz de Dominguez. She's more attractive in that big statue in the park than in this mask. I didn't know you and John had been to Queretaro."

"I haven't. John went a number of years ago to look at some obscure ruins in the Sierra Gorda and, of course, stopped in Queretaro. He fell in love with the beautiful colonial buildings. He wasn't usually interested in anything more recent than the Conquest but the Corregidora's house and the little plaza it looks out upon caught his fancy. He thought it the most perfect square he'd seen in Mexico. He planned to take me there."

Maude chortled. "I started to invite you to go with me. I'm afraid John and I both let you down. Take yourself there."

"Maude this is unnerving. One moment we're having a light conversation and the next moment we are back facing death. It's macabre."

"I know. It's been happening to me ever since I made the decision. I'd be planning the party and then it would hit me. Here." Maude laid a hand over her heart. "Or in the pit of my stomach. That's one reason I asked you to rush down—to distract me. You have to promise we won't mention this again until after the party. As Ma used to say, 'Just let it lay where Jesus flang it.'"

Sydney smiled sadly. "All right. That is the most provocative quote. It always puzzles me, and amuses me. I remember the first time I heard you use it. Pearson had just been killed in Vietnam and I was agonizing over what does it all mean and you advised, 'Let it lay where Jesus flang it, as Ma used to say.' I didn't know whether to laugh or cry."

"I promise you Darlin' that the party will take your mind off everything else. It's going to be a real fiesta.

"You'll see lots of Pancho Villas and Zapatas. Several presidents of Mexico. Plenty of personalities from the States because many of the guests are from north of the border. Jack Kennedy. And Jackie. Bill, or maybe Hillary. Chelsea would be imaginative. Elvis for sure. Madonna's a good bet. You can count on a few birds. Jungle cats. Several bulls, that ubiquitous symbol of strength in this country."

"And you?"

"That's a surprise. It will amuse you I promise. I may have made one mistake when I planned the perfect party. Weeks ago when I reserved the restaurant for December 12 it didn't occur to me that it was the final night of the Virgin of Guadalupe celebration. I had already sent invitations when it dawned on me. There will be mobs in the street and traffic will be impossible but maybe all the excitement will add to the festive air. Have you ever been here for Guadalupe days?"

"No, but I was in Oaxaca once and I remember the processions were wonderful. They went on for days. The last night there were Indians in from the villages wearing splendid, colorful regalia and dancing in the streets and in the churches"

"There will be fireworks around town but not so elaborate as ours at the end of the evening. It will be nice that thousands can enjoy the display, not just those of us partying at the cafe."

"Maude how can you enjoy a party with what you're planning?"

"You've broken your promise." She winked. "How can you not enjoy a party when you know it's your last one?"

Alfonso parked the car at the edge of the cobbled street just at the foot of steep steps.

Sydney looked up. "I can tell it's going to be a delight just from the sign and the colorful collage under it. Look at the darling bar on the deck." She glanced down to Maude who had paused there to rest three steps below. "Need a hand?"

"No, thanks. I'll be all right in a minute."

Sydney waited and they walked together through the wide open doors.

"Oh," Sydney gasped. "You're right. It's so happy. It is magical. I love that lavender wall and the old rose tablecloths with white chairs against the *tromp l'oeil* blue sky and the fluffy clouds. I love. . . ." She laughed and turned to Maude. "What a spectacular setting for a party!"

A short, muscular, excessively good-looking young man stepped away from the bar where he had been watching them.

"Hi. You must be Sydney." Wheat-colored hair fell over his brow in a contrived but attractive way. "Wait until you see the garden. That's my favorite area. There's a stream running through and all sorts of bright-colored contemporary art."

"You can't be anyone other than Hale," Sydney said when he paused for breath.

He nodded and with a smile motioned them to chairs around a table near the bar.

"I took the liberty of ordering. Maude told me you favor Johnny Walker Black over ice with just a splash. I'll join you. We all know for Maude it has to be a martini." With his elbows on the table he leaned forward companionably as they clicked glasses.

"*Salud*," Maude said. "Hale is right about the garden. There's another lavender wall as you start up toward the terrace and a tall white wall where the plaster is peeled off artistically in spots and there are wrought iron sun faces scattered around. It sounds too well thought out but it works. With your good eye you'll love it. Tables are arranged on different levels and the same pretty cloths. Gorgeous greenery. You'll see. We'll go out there in a while."

"Why haven't you brought me here before? It's enchanting."

"You never stay long enough. You always insist on one of Panchita's great dinners and we walk over to Le Bistro one night for the jazz and their good food and the next day you're gone."

"I'm sure Maude has told you," Hale said, changing the subject abruptly. "I hope you've come to dissuade her."

"Hale," Maude said sternly. "You promised."

Hale Howard put his drink down and clenched his fist, then brought it down hard on the table. "Sydney, you can't let her."

Startled, it was a moment before Sydney spoke. "Hale, I can't." She reached across the table and took her friend's hand. "If Maude has made up her mind then I've come to help her." It was the first time she had stated her resolve but she had known what she was compelled to do since Maude called her in Santa Fe. "I hope you will too."

Maude lifted her glass. "Thank you Darlin'." She then set it on the table and, still holding Sydney's hand, reached with her other hand for Hale. "Now look, I'm thinking we'll put the table for champagne over there." She turned back toward the entrance. "I'm going to sit on a high stool just in front of the piano. I'll be wearing black and the white grand with the lid full open will complement my costume. I want you two to stand beside me."

They began to protest.

"No. It's settled. For a party you want your bestest friends near you and you two are them. There will be food tables in each room and several places in the garden."

"What kind of food?"

"Delectable. They've won all sorts of awards. When the place is written up they always talk about a blend of provincial Mexican flavors with classical French cuisine, whatever that is. What they can do with fish and chicken is wondrous."

"And beef," Hale added. "One of the famous places in Mexico for beef."

"You'll find out just how superb the food is tomorrow night," Maude promised.

"How will the guests know who you are—who we are—as we greet them if we're wearing masks?" Hale asked.

"Most of them won't know Sydney but I expect they'll recognize you and me, Hale, even with our faces covered. I've thought about that. It will be fun to wear masks, at least for a while. Then we can take them off and mingle."

They followed Maude to the next room as she explained details to members of the restaurant staff. She pointed out where the mariachis would stand and where they would clear a space for dancing. Hale strolled between the two tall women seeming at ease with his five feet four. He held Maude's arm as they climbed the steps to the garden and suggested they sit while they talked. A waiter appeared immediately and placed their drinks on the table.

"What time is the party Maude?"

"Nine o'clock. The Anglos will come right on time. The Mexicans will arrive around ten or ten-thirty. I want everyone in the garden or out on the entrance deck for the fireworks. That will end the party at midnight. I want to be sure Alfonso is here with the car then."

"He'll be here. The police escort is all arranged," Hale assured her.

"I'll be bushed by then."

"I'll be zonked. I think I shall drink champagne rather than Scotch."

"Well now, you're getting caught up in the spirit as I was sure you would."

"I know," Sydney admitted. "I can't resist a party."

"Maude has told us that a fortune teller predicted you would outlive three husbands," Valenciana Tello was saying. "And you have. She says you are superstitious. Not to wonder."

"Jesus, Maude." Sydney tried to keep her voice light. "What else have you told your Vallarta friends?"

"That your slight limp is the result of having been tossed over a balcony in London by a handsome lover." Julia Lundgren's blue eyes sparkled. "I must say we found that dramatic and traumatic and romantic."

Sydney laughed tentatively. "It was certainly traumatic. Perhaps dramatic. Not all that romantic I can assure you. And, it is stretching to call him a lover. He *was* handsome though," she acknowledged and took a sip of Scotch.

Sydney was sitting on the deck at Le Bistro with Maude and friends.

"I want you to meet my probably closest friends here in Vallarta," Maude had said over breakfast. "Sometimes I think we see too much of one another. We bicker a bit. We're not all that close but they're good company. And I think, all in all, they're true blue. They've heard so much about you. Julia has met you but Valenciana and Edwina haven't.

"I'm not quite up to par today so I think I'll rest until lunch. See you about one o'clock. I always like to go out for lunch when I'm having a party in the evening, don't you?" she said over her shoulder as she left the room.

"You taught me that," Sydney admitted. "And now I do. But most hostesses are fretting over the party around noon."

"No need to fret in this case. Everything is ready."

Promptly at one Maude appeared. "Feeling rested," she announced.

Eloisa opened the door and Corn followed them to the car, his lead dragging behind. He stood patiently while they settled in the back seat and then jumped into the front.

"Is Corn going to lunch?"

"Yes. He loves Le Bistro. Don't ask me why. All he does is stretch out on the deck and snore. There's a marvelous pale orange cat that hangs around there and at first Corn wanted to chase it. The cat stepped through the grill and sat on the ledge above the river knowing it was out of reach. After a few attempts to thrust his big head between the wrought iron bars Corn figured out it was wasted effort so now he just reclines immediately. I notice he raises his head if a waiter proffers a bite."

Maude offered another drink and Sydney decided it was in order considering the drift of the conversation.

"Maude says you were an actress and that you are addicted to diamonds and emeralds and if times are lean you just make payments," Valenciana laughed. "You are my kind of customer. I wish I had more like you in my shop."

"Is there anything you've forgotten to tell them?" Sydney turned to Maude, teasing, but with a slight edge in her voice.

"Oh yes, lots Darlin'."

"I must say the bits and pieces of information she has given us all add up to make you glamorous and a little mysterious," Julia explained.

"Hi." Hale strode across the deck and kissed Maude and then the other three. He leaned down to pet Corn. His hand paused on Sydney's shoulder in a casual but affectionate gesture. "Sorry to bother you at lunch Maude but I need you to look at something if I can lure you away for a few moments."

Maude excused herself and followed him back into the big bar at the entrance.

Valenciana looked around to be certain Maude was out of earshot. "Is Maude all right? We're worried."

Sydney swallowed but did not hesitate before replying. "I'd say she's fine from that laugh we just heard from the bar. And from the second martini she ordered," she added. "Why do you ask?"

"She cancelled lunch at the last moment a couple of weeks ago."

Julia took the lead. "And that's not like her."

"Doctor Rodriguez has been to the house twice during the night within the past weeks." Edwina wanted to share in providing information.

"Who's Doctor Rodriguez?"

"He's the one we all use here in Vallarta. General practitioner. Very competent." Julia smiled. "He will make house calls. Especially after you reach a certain age. He came to the hotel when I had laryngitis the first week I arrived. Age wouldn't explain his going to call on Maude though. And in the middle of the night?"

"How do you know about the house calls?"

Valenciana leaned forward and beamed. "Oh, *everyone* knows *everything* that goes on around here," she said easily.

"Good. I'm glad. Doctor Rodriguez is quite something. When he came to see about my laryngitis I told him I'm going to be eighty soon. I told him I find myself telling people that. He smiled ever so gently and said a curious thing happens. One is suddenly proud of having lived so long. Almost overnight it seems a worthwhile accomplishment. He took it lightly. Just patted my hand and changed the subject and I felt much better."

"Julia," Valenciana said sharply. "You're drifting. I think you're in danger of becoming a professional *old* woman."

"That was unkind and unnecessary," Edwina scolded. "I've been concerned about Maude because she hasn't walked Corn on the beach for a good while. When I questioned her she was vague and said Alfonso liked to walk with him. When I offered to take him she just turned it off. You know Maude. . . ."

"Now, what do you know about Maude?" She snickered as she returned to the table. "I'm back. Hale is going to join us for a drink."

How nice to have Hale with them, Sydney thought. She turned her attention to his casual chatter and shook off a sudden heaviness.

Three unicorns pranced gracefully on the sidewalk at the foot of the steps leading up to Café des Artistes. As Maude and Sydney and Hale approached, the lead beast leaned over and brushed his white muzzle against Maude's cheek and with one agile movement lifted her in his arms and danced around and up the stairs. His two partners turned somersaults on the steps and did handstands on the rails as Maude was placed gently on the porch in front of the door.

Sydney, Hale, and a dozen other early arrivals, applauded from the sidewalk as Maude waved and disappeared through the wide doors.

"I take it that was planned to make the entrance easy." Sydney looked at Hale. "It certainly seemed spontaneous but Maude has rested a couple of times today and driving over she said she'd be glad when the party's over and she can just go to bed."

"Of course it was planned. Wasn't it splendid! One of the disturbing things about Maude's condition is that sometimes she is her old self and then again she has no energy. She'll rise to the occasion. You know how a party excites her."

"Who are the dancers?"

"A local team called Unicorns Three. They entertain for lots of her parties and she's gotten them booked into all sorts of places in the States. We told them she wanted to make a theatrical entrance and they were happy to oblige."

Hale and Sydney paused on the landing with compliments and the three bowed deeply. Light shimmered on their fawn-colored body suits as they each turned a somersault and, one after the other, descended the stairs on their hands. Everyone clapped.

Maude was waiting for them in front of the piano. Hale reached into the large shopping bag he was carrying and pulled out a head. "Here." He handed it to Sydney. "I'm not tall enough to put it on for her."

"The Corn Dog," Sydney exclaimed. "It's perfect. You said I'd be amused. It's as light as a feather."

"Fiberglass, Darlin'. How does it look?"

"Great!" they agreed in unison.

Sydney settled the ornate, intricately carved collar onto Maude's shoulders. The tongue of the ancient dog hung down between two rows of sharp, strong-looking teeth and he seemed to be smiling mischievously.

"Maude, we might have known you would do something outrageous."

A glorious white peacock hugged the dog but was careful not to disturb its plumage.

"Valenciana, step back and let me look at you." Maude's friend turned slowly revealing the feathers secured to her white mini-skirt. "I said it wasn't necessary to wear more than a mask but I'm glad you did. You really dress the party. I love that."

Immediately Maude was surrounded by a crowd that included Diego Rivera and Frida Kahlo, Shirley Temple, Dennis Rodman, two Pancho Villas, a jaguar and a pelican. Hale and Sydney were standing to one side holding their masks. "Let's get a drink and watch the show. Now that she's holding court she'll not even miss us." Hale led the way to the bar and they perched on stools to enjoy the parade.

"Oh look," Sydney pointed. "That must be Miss Marple."

"Really. You could have fooled me."

"Obviously you are not an Agatha Christie fan. Who is that gorgeous creature?"

"Where?"

"Moving slowly through the door."

"That's Dolores Del Rio tonight, but I don't know who it is in real life. I can't see the legs."

"There aren't any legs. She's wearing a long full skirt of many bright colors."

"You're right. I couldn't see that far down through the crowd."

"How did you happen to recognize her?"

"I watch old movies and she's popular down here."

"I read that one reason she was so beautiful was that she slept sixteen hours a day."

"How did you know about that?"

"I'm good at non-essential information. Sometimes not so good at important details."

"I can add to your stock of trivia. Did you know that there is a statue of Dolores Del Rio in Chapultepec Park?"

"You're teasing me."

"No. I swear. The next time you're in Mexico City go look." He thought for a moment. "Or is it Marilyn Monroe?"

"You're not such an avid pursuer of trivia as you think or you would be more precise." Sydney laughed.

"No, but I'd make a bet that you'll check me out to see which one."

"I'll let you know."

Suddenly, the strains of a waltz floated from the next room.

"Let's put on our heads and go dancing."

"Zapata! What fun. I noticed you were all in white but I thought you were just being tropical. You look exactly like Zapata in the Rivera mural in Cuernavaca."

"That's the idea. Glad you recognize me."

"Except for the white horse."

"He's waiting outside. Come, Doña Josefa."

"Oh, I won't be a surprise. Maude told you I was going to be the Corregidora."

"She was so pleased with your mask—and with hers—that she couldn't wait. You are right to be clad in black but Doña Josefa would be shocked by the bare arms and the deep V front and back."

"I had planned to wear a divine new Helmut Lang pantsuit, almost the same color as the unicorns' body suits, but when I discovered who I'd be portraying I opted for black. Doña Josefa Ortiz de Dominguez and Emiliano Zapata—not bad dancing partners," Sydney whispered as they moved onto the crowded floor.

By the time they had finished the waltz, a tango, a rhumba, and conversation with a leopard, a Chac-Mool and Jack Kennedy, Maude had moved into the garden followed by flocks of guests.

"I haven't danced this much since my accident several years ago. I may pay tomorrow but it was much fun tonight," Sydney said and performed a stylish pirouette.

"I've saved seats for you." Maude motioned for Sydney and Hale. They carefully removed their heads and placed them on the table beside the Corn Dog and sat down. "Glad you two enjoyed the dancing. That's what parties are for. And for drinking," she added as a waiter replaced her empty glass with a fresh martini. She turned to Hale. "What time is it?"

"Almost eleven. You O.K.?"

"Not great. Another hour. I can make it if I sit. Have you seen Julia?"

"No, now that you ask."

"I'm concerned. She promised. In fact, she was looking forward to the evening."

Elizabeth Taylor was moving toward them. Not the Elizabeth from *National Velvet* or even *Who's Afraid of Virginia Woolf*. But Taylor, still beautiful, looking like the recent tabloid photos.

"Edwina how could you?" Maude laughed. "You're bad."

"Well she's my neighbor. At least her house is. My body wouldn't work with her face when she was in *A Place in the Sun* or *Giant* so I decided on this."

"You're unforgivable. Have you seen Julia?"

"No, but I was late. Who is she impersonating?"

"She wouldn't tell me. She just said it would be a surprise."

"The food looks wonderful." Sydney moved closer to the table.

"It is. Absolutely superb," Edwina assured her. "Though I had trouble eating through the mask."

Sydney was just finishing the delectable salmon when Maude asked Hale to pass the word that it was almost time for fireworks. "Everyone needs to be on the porch by the bar or here in the garden to see the display."

As Hale started to leave he suddenly turned back. "Here comes Dolores Del Rio. Let's see who she is."

The gorgeous creature, as Sydney had described her, moved leisurely through the crowd, stopping frequently to chat. The wide skirt of multi-colored ruffles swayed sensuously with each step. She was covered from neck to waist in folds of soft white chiffon. As she arrived, she leaned down and brushed Maude's cheek, whispering a greeting in Spanish.

"*Buenas tardes Señorita Del Rio,*" Maude replied.

"And I thought *salud* was your only Spanish word," Sydney quipped.

Dolores Del Rio lifted her mask and became Julia Lundgren, laughing heartily. "Not one person recognized me. Quite a *coup*, wouldn't you say?"

"How did you choose that wonderful dress?"

"I think it's what she wore for *Flying Down to Rio*."

"Marvelous Julia!" Maude congratulated her friend. "Everyone recognized me, even wearing my mask."

"Of course," Edwina said matter-of-factly. "Who else would appear as the Corn Dog?"

"Come on everyone." Hale was shepherding guests, mostly unmasked, into the garden.

The drummer from the rock group on the porch began to beat off the seconds. At the stroke of midnight mariachi trumpets blared and whistling rockets streaked through the air.

There were stars and fountains and then HAIL HALE materialized in bright block letters. As colorful sparks drifted toward the ground they were replaced by horizontal wheels and waterfalls. Then

VIVA VAL
JOY JULIA
SUPER SYDNEY
WINNING EDWINA
CUTE CORN
BEAUTIFUL BABY

lit up the sky.

Other greetings, in groups of six or eight, spread rapidly across the night. Guests squealed with delight as their names appeared and rounds of applause greeted the bold splash of stars that filled the wide black expanse.

There was a pause and everyone slowly crowded toward Maude to say goodnight.

Three whistling rockets shot up and giant white, green and red letters spelled out BYE DARLIN'S.

"Can Alfonso get any closer? I hate to push through this mob all the way down the block." Maude paused and took a deep breath. Sydney was carrying all three masks in Hale's shopping bag. She could feel weight on the arm she had linked through Maude's.

"Stupid," Hale muttered. "The police car, instead of being in front to clear a path, is following your car. You two will do better single file I think. I'm going to see if I can get the car any nearer. Here." He reached for the bag. "I'll take the masks. Don't try to rush. Just move as you can."

"How many people are there here?" Sydney asked as they inched forward.

"Thousands and thousands around town. What would you say, five thousand in this block. At least most are moving in the same direction."

"Everyone is so courteous," Sydney observed as there was a slight opening for a couple trying to walk against the crowd.

The Unicorns Three came up beside them. "We'll try to clear the way," one of them screamed as they pushed ahead. In seconds they were swallowed up in the undulating wave of people.

Hale managed to make his way back.

"How far to the car?" Maude questioned as he hugged her and asked if she was all right.

"Still half a block."

"If I can only sit down," Maude gasped.

"I'm trying to get as close as I can." He disappeared back into the swarm.

"Here. Let me put my arm around you, under your arms. That may help." As Sydney struggled to raise her arm Maude began to slump. "Jesus, if you fall we'll be trampled. *Ayudeme! Ayudeme! Por favor.* Help me." No response. The throng moved around them as she managed to ease Maude to the sidewalk. Sydney knelt, trying to shield her from the sea of moving feet.

One of the unicorns appeared. He got to his knees beside Sydney, raising his voice, hoping to be heard above the din. "We couldn't see you. What happened?"

Sydney leaned toward him. "I don't know. She gasped. And then collapsed."

He picked Maude up gently. The other two unicorns joined him, yelling, and parted the crowd. Sydney rushed through the opening.

Hale spotted them as they neared the car. "My god, what happened?" he shouted.

"I don't know. She just crumpled."

"I'll take her," Hale insisted.

The unicorn placed Maude in his arms.

Sydney turned to the beast. "You're covered with blood!"

He pointed. "You too but it doesn't show much on black."

The crowd quieted somewhat and cleared a path. Hale walked past Maude's car to a police vehicle. "Open the door," he said to the unicorn. "And help me get her in. To the hospital," he commanded the police car driver. "Move it. I don't care how many you run down."

"May I come?" the unicorn asked.

"No. Better not. To the hospital," he repeated. "Move. Goddamn it."

Lights were flashing and the siren blared as a policeman on foot tried to clear a space, blowing a whistle and waving his arms. Curious, the mob closed in to see what was happening.

In spite of the crush, the patrol car driver managed to get around Maude's car and edge forward. Sydney quickly climbed into the front seat of the Cadillac beside Alfonso. "See if you can follow the police."

"Are you all right Señora?"

"I'm fine Alfonso but something terrible has happened to Señora Maude."

"May I get in?" a tall young man with a southern accent asked Alfonso. His body suit was blood soaked and he was holding a unicorn head.

"Please. Get in." Sydney leaned forward so he could climb into the back seat.

Alfonso hit the gas, but even with his agile driving, they lost the police car ahead of them.

"Can't you go any faster?" the unicorn asked impatiently. "Of course you can't," he instantly answered his own question.

"You're from the States," Sydney said. "Judging from the accent and the blonde hair."

"Georgia," he admitted. "We're all three from Atlanta. But we sure like the beach and the girls and all the people here. Thanks to Señora Maude's help we're doing well. I hope she's all right."

They roared up to the hospital entrance. There was not a sound, nor a soul, in the lobby.

"I'll try that hall," Sydney said.

But before she could reach the door, Hale burst in.

"She's dead! Maude's dead Sydney. Stabbed. She bled to death."

He was no longer the swaggering revolutionary Zapata of the party. His spotless white costume was now stained and blood was drying in his usually carefully coiffed hair where he had run a hand across his forehead.

Sydney, stunned, stepped toward him.

"What are we going to do?" he murmured.

"I don't know Hale. I don't know what we're going to do." She eased forward and touched his arm.

He jerked away. "Leave me alone." And before any of them could react he ran from the building.

A nurse appeared . "What happened?" Sydney questioned.

"We do not know. The police are here. I hope we will know something tomorrow morning."

"You can't tell us anything?"

"No. I'm sorry. We do not know how it happened. The police do not know. They have said we must not talk to anyone while they are investigating. I'm sorry," she repeated as she turned away.

Sydney put one hand on Alfonso's shoulder and the other on the arm of the tall, blonde unicorn. "May we drop you somewhere?"

"Thanks. If you could get me back where I can look for my buddies. Will Hale be all right?"

"I don't know. Where did he go?"

He shrugged. "No idea. We'll try to find him."

Neither Sydney nor Alfonso spoke on the slow drive home.

"Thank you Alfonso. We'll talk first thing in the morning." She shivered. Maude would say a rabbit ran over her grave, she thought. "There will be many things to do tomorrow."

Alfonso nodded. "Good-night Señora."

Sydney hurried to the telephone and rang Hale's house. No answer. She sighed and, exhausted, sat down on the portal in an *equipal* chair and put her head in her hands.

Maude is dead. What could have happened? I come here to be with my dear friend under circumstances too dreadful for words, and now she's murdered. At least she didn't have to take her own life. But this can't be a better solution. Or can it?

The big dog rubbed against her leg. Sydney, hearing his whimper, raised her head and touched her forehead to his as she began to cry. Corn moved closer and with his black tongue licked away the tears.

"Oh, Jesus," Sydney whispered as she cradled the broad head in her hands. "I think we're stuck with one another."

*H*ale pulled out a chair as Sydney walked across the deck toward the lagoon-side table. "Thanks for joining me."

"Another pretty restaurant. Vallarta has more than its share. The colors are delightful and the food so good. It's sinful." She looked up. "And we have a canopy of trees to shade us."

"I want to apologize, as I said on the phone yesterday, for falling apart. I just couldn't imagine life without Maude." His voice broke. "Still can't."

"Neither can I. I was worried about you. I called the house. There was no answer and I didn't know what to do."

"Sorry. I walked on the beach for a long time. Then I went home and got drunk. I had a hell of a hangover yesterday but I think I'm together enough to take care of business now. Somehow it didn't seem right to meet in some office to talk about what's to be done. Maude would like us to be here on the Isla enjoying food and drink. I took the liberty of ordering Johnny Walker Black."

"Thanks."

"And a double for me."

The drinks arrived promptly. "Do you wish to order Señor Hale?"

"Not just yet." He turned to Sydney. "Do we?"

"No hurry. Maude would remind you that you called this meeting. So begin. Have you heard from the police?"

"Not yet."

"Maude said you'd been friends forever and been through a lot and she knew she could always count on you."

"We went through field hockey and trying to copy from one another on quizzes and winding the Maypole. Since those childhood days she's helped me through the loss of three husbands and I was with her for her emotional and complicated divorce from Bob."

"She told me she was calling you to come down. I told her no one would help her end her own life. But she was certain that you would. I told her if you couldn't I would. I'm not sure I meant it. I may have just been carried away by the emotion of the moment. Now it's all academic."

"How did you and Maude connect? She mentioned you often but I never asked."

"You know that old cliché about so and so changed my life. I'm afraid I've picked up a lot of trite sayings from Maude. Anyhow, Maude changed my life dramatically. I had a law degree but never practiced. I'm also a CPA and I was working for a big accounting firm and they assigned me to a project for Maude. You know how she was. She'd ask a few questions and before you knew it you had told her your entire life story.

"It was about time for her to come to Vallarta and she invited me to come along and spend a week in the guest house.

"Mostly we went out for breakfast, lunch and dinner. Now and then we stayed in and enjoyed one of Panchita's superb dishes. In a few days I was getting to like having a Bloody Mary for breakfast while listening to a piano player and chatting about inane topics. There was a big opening at Pacifico and I met lots of fun people. Maude had what she called 'a little get-together' for about fifty or so. I liked everybody and they seemed to like me. I got a kick out of walking out the front door to go swimming in the ocean. I was sunburned and hadn't worn socks for a week. Then it was time to go.

"'Don't,' she said.

"'I have to.'

"'Why?'

"'I should go back to my job.'

"'Nonsense. Forget your job. You're not an accountant at heart. You're a playboy. I can tell.'

"'I have to make a living. What do I do here?'

"'Work for me. I can use a lawyer. And lots of my friends need one from time to time. A good Gringo lawyer can do well down here.'

"'I've never practiced law. How do you know I'll be any good?'

"'I can tell, Darlin'. The first thing you have to do is change your name. You need a fun name.'

"And that was how it was. I won't give you all the details. You know how Maude managed things and you hardly realized what was happening."

"Don't I just." Sydney laughed. "Did you change your name?"

"Sort of. I protested, thinking it was affected. But Maude said half the people she knew were affected. She said I was going to be a dashing, successful lawyer. Of course I was embarrassed and laughed. My name was Howard Hale. She said Howard was an accountant's name and suggested we reverse it. So, I became Hale Howard. And that was the end of the discussion."

"Do you like practicing law?"

"I do. I'm good at it, if I do say so myself, to borrow another of Maude's clichés. At first I had several clients but over time Maude gave me more and more responsibility and eventually I worked just for her. Her affairs were complex and challenging. I dealt with a couple of long-time attorneys in the States. One firm went back to the days when the family first struck oil. But mostly Maude called the shots from here."

"What did you do when Maude went back home?"

"I was still based here but I was back and forth all the time doing things for her."

"How long has this been?"

"Almost three years. So much has changed in my life that it seems like at least a dozen."

"I know I've been here since you began working for her. I remember seeing your name on some house papers. She spoke of you so I feel I've known you. I was totally occupied with construction details during the building and then John was killed and I haven't been here but once since.

"Maude was wonderful," Sydney mused. "She would just drop in casually in Santa Fe when she sensed I needed shoring up. And we met from time to time in New York and on the west coast but I've missed my visits to Vallarta. What will you do now?"

"Maude and I talked a good bit about it since we've been working out the details due to her dreadful idea of committing suicide. I'll stay here after all this business is concluded. I need your help."

"A question before we go into that. Is Maude to be buried here? Returned home? What's to be done?"

"She's being cremated. I was already figuring out the paper work. You can imagine how much red tape there is when a U.S. citizen dies here, especially if it's murder. She wanted the ashes taken to Italy."

"I know where. San Gimignano."

"You're absolutely right. How did you know?"

"She and Bob rented a little place there for a month, a couple of times early on. I visited them once."

"She said it was the happiest time of their life together."

"They had a marvelous place that had views. I suppose every house in San Gimignano has a view. I told them my only reservation was that before you looked out across the Tuscan landscape you looked down on a cemetery in the foreground. Maude said that was where she wanted to be buried. We all laughed, thinking we'd never die."

"That's the place. And, are you ready? You and I are to take the ashes. She thinks the same priest who was there may still be around to help with arrangements. He was young then, she said."

"She does still manage things, even from afar. Is there a date for this pilgrimage?"

"No. When all the investigations are over and at our convenience, which is thoughtful. But she gave me plenty of instructions—where we are to stay in Florence, what kind of car we are to rent. Which are the most desirable rooms at La Cisterna."

Sydney nodded affectionately. "First things first. Maude said I should stand by you and help in any way I could. I'm here to do that."

Hale stood up slowly and looked down at Sydney. He then walked over to the deck railing and stared at the still water. When he turned back his eyes were glistening.

"Thank you. I'm going to need that. Most of all with the children. Maude said Rob would be angry and petulant and make no effort to hide his feelings. She then laughed and said Lucy would be comforted by money but I know she will be really shaken."

"Those were Maude's exact words to me."

"I called Lucy in the small hours of yesterday morning before I got too drunk. She was calm but devastated. I offered to call Rob but she said she'd better do that. They're meeting in Houston and flying down together. They'll be in around six and are coming directly to my office. Rob wants the will read at once. I would like you to be there."

"Of course."

"Let me fill you in on the general terms of the will and about arrangements for the 'final little get-together' as Maude called it."

Sydney shook her head. "There'll not be another like her for a long while. Does the fact that she was murdered change anything?"

"Not so far as the funeral goes since she had already made plans in preparation for this little get-together. Actually, I think the kids and her friends can deal better with the thought of murder than they could have with suicide.

"A party, she instructed. No scripture. No speeches. No singing hymns. The children are the principal beneficiaries. You and I are named. And, you get the Corn Dog," he added playfully.

"I'm happy to have him," Sydney said softly. "I told him that the other evening."

"Good. How did he react?"

"He just yawned and went to sleep."

Hale gave her a broad grin. "A couple of her long-time attorneys are mentioned. Dr. Rodriguez gets to open an outpatient clinic he's dreamed about forever. All the household staff. Bob gets that wonderful Pissarro that hangs in the bedroom. Turns out they bought it for their tenth anniversary. Julia Lundgren will have a big Marta Gilbert painting that she's always liked and Edwina and Valenciana have each been left a handsome piece of jewelry. I'm to dispose of her personal belongings as I see fit after the children and you choose whatever you like. It's a straightforward will for a person with so much. Oh, the local Friendship Club has been remembered with a donation to their cleft-palate fund and there are a number of charities in the States."

He stopped abruptly.

"There is one thing more I should tell you in good conscience."

Sydney looked at him quizzically. "Oh?"

"Maude left me not only the house but, in my view, loads of money. There is an additional odd provision. We were out on a boat in the bay with friends early on, when I had just begun to manage her affairs, and there was a sudden storm. I thought, I'm sure we all thought, we were going to drown. The next day she called and told me to look at her insurance policy. It had an unusual provision for an extra million if she were killed in some strange accident that might be considered an Act of God. 'I thought last night was going to be that accident,' she said with a giggle. 'Or if I am murdered. It was a come-on gimmick and didn't cost anything extra and I thought it was amusing.' We both laughed. 'Anyhow, in either of those extreme cases I want to leave the extra million to you.' I thanked her, we had it put in the will, and I never thought of it again until now." He shrugged.

"You won't believe me if I pretend I'm not startled."

"Of course. But there it is." He changed the subject. "More about the get-together. It will be at seven o'clock—A.M.—morning. At Le Bistro."

Sydney groaned. "I hate the time but I love the place."

"Maude said you would be appalled by the hour. She said you consider anything before noon early. There will be piano music and Bloody Marys, champagne, margaritas—anything you can think of to drink—you name it.

"The food will be unbelievable. That's what we were doing when I pulled her away from you at lunch. She chose her favorites from breakfast, lunch and dinner. Those delectable fruits and breads, crepes and quiche. Spinach enchiladas and, in case there are hearty eaters around at that hour, she selected Shrimp Portugues and Chicken Voiture Au Rose de Salmon. I won't even try to describe the sweets."

"I'm not sure about such a lavish breakfast at that ungodly hour. How did she set this up? Did she give them a date?"

"No. She just went over everything on the phone and said she'd get back to them with time and date. But she mentioned that it would be early in the day.

"Yesterday I explained that we wanted to carry out her wishes. If the hour surprised them it was not apparent.

"Here's the kicker. Every mourner who shows up at that early hour gets ten thousand dollars. Maude predicted there would be fifteen max."

"I predict more than twice that."

"I agree. Every bartender or waiter on duty will get five hundred dollars."

Sydney shook her head and smiled. "Maude. Maude."

*H*ale moved easily around the desk, a sheaf of papers in his hands. He joined Lucy and Rob and Sydney who were seated in comfortable chairs arranged around a handsome eighteenth-century table.

Sydney glanced around the office and detected Maude's fine hand—the dark paneled walls, expensive furniture that might have been appropriate in New York or London or San Francisco, the impressive library. She would wager there were not many similar law offices in Vallarta.

"Would you like tea? Or coffee?" He checked his watch. "Actually, it's drink time. What may I offer you? Johnny Walker Black. Easy on the water," he said, smiling at Sydney.

She nodded.

"Let me guess." He turned affably to Lucy. "Chivas and water?"

"Nothing for me," Rob said sharply. "This is not a social situation. Let's get on with it."

A young woman in a white uniform who had been waiting unobtrusively by the door glided away.

"Your mother was generous to you and to a number of others," Hale began.

Sydney had seen Hale only in casual slacks and sneakers or khaki shorts and a cotton sweater, and his Zapata costume. Now he was wearing a dark year-round-weight suit of the finest wool. His collar was starched; gold cuff links were monogrammed. His silk tie no doubt had a designer label.

"How great. To whom?" Rob asked.

"First to you and your sister." Hale glanced at Rob and Sydney could tell he was irritated. "You will receive twelve million dollars with a bonus of two million because your mother felt you had made exceptionally wise investments for her during the past years."

"I'm glad she appreciated that fact."

Hale faced Lucy across the table.

"And to you she left twelve million."

"I can't believe it! I thought Ma would consider me irresponsible and would put everything in a trust fund so I wouldn't blow it." Lucy raised her hands above her head in a victory salute and shouted, "Thank you Ma!"

"Lucy calm down. We'll talk. I'll invest for you so you won't be a bartender all your life."

"Like hell we'll talk Rob. I'll do any damn thing I want. It's my money."

"We shall see."

Hale cleared his throat in a studied way that made Sydney smile to herself. The drinks arrived. He turned to Rob. "Are you sure you won't have something?"

"No. Keep going."

"Maude," Hale said, and he paused for a moment. "Maude left the house and three million to me." He stopped, enjoying the impact he knew this information was having.

It took a moment for Rob to believe what he had heard and then he spurted out, "She can't do that. You're her lawyer."

"All this was arranged by her attorney in Mexico City, Alfredo Lopez-Gomez. Everything is in order I assure you. As you will see from these papers."

Lucy jumped to her feet. "I'm thrilled for you Hale." She hugged him warmly. "You were so good to Ma. And so good for her. I'm glad."

"Don't you think you're overreacting Lucy?"

"Oh, Rob, you're such a prick."

"What else?" Rob asked, dreading the answer.

"There is an unusual provision in her life insurance policy. It states that if she met accidental death under extreme circumstances, such as an Act of God, the policy paid an additional million." Before Rob could respond he added, "Or if she was murdered. That million comes to me."

Rob sank into his chair and shook his head slowly. Sydney thought he was going to explode. She felt uncomfortable, knowing she was on the list for his anger.

Hale then moved away from the group and positioned himself in the big chair behind his desk and shuffled the papers. "Sydney is to get nine hundred thousand in cash and the Cadillac."

"She doesn't need money," Rob blurted. "That makes a million including that ridiculous car that cost Ma a bundle. Close to a hundred thousand."

Sydney faced Rob with her wide, enchanting smile. "Isn't it nice to have someone give you something you don't really need. How like your mother."

If Sydney had been surprised it was not apparent, Hale thought with admiration. "And she gets the Corn Dog."

"Thank god we don't have to deal with that beast. What other ridiculous bequests did she make?"

"Not ridiculous. She remembered Kera with two hundred thousand and she is leaving something to everyone who worked at the house—ten thousand each to Alfonso and Panchita. Lesser amounts to the others. Her special friends down here, Julia and Valenciana and Edwina, are getting jewelry and, in Julia's case, a painting. There is a bequest of one hundred thousand to the Friendship Club to help with their cleft-palate program."

"Cleft-palate program," Rob muttered. "What else?"

"Doctor Rodriguez will receive two hundred thousand to set up the clinic he has always envisioned. A number of charities in the States are named. The amount they each receive depends upon what is left after all commitments. It will be sizable."

"Any other surprises?"

"Just one. Anyone who turns up at the service tomorrow morning at Le Bistro at seven o'clock will get ten thousand dollars. Bartenders and waiters are being given five hundred each. That's part of the commitments."

"This is absurd. She must have taken leave of her senses. How could she have decided to give people money for coming to her funeral when she didn't know she was going to die?"

Hale looked to Sydney for help.

"Rob," she said calmly, "she knew she was going to die. She was planning to do it herself. That's why I'm here."

"You knew she was going to kill herself and you weren't going to stop her. And you consider yourself a friend?"

"Just a minute!" Hale interrupted.

"It's all right Hale."

"Why?" Lucy asked in a quiet voice.

"Her heart was badly damaged. The only hope was a transplant and that was not certain. Anyhow, she was too old to be a likely candidate for the operation," Sydney added.

"Too old?" Lucy got up and eased over to Sydney. She slowly sat on the floor and put her head in Sydney's lap. "Too old? She wouldn't have been fifty until next summer."

"I know."

"How awful for you to know all that."

"Not so awful as for her. I didn't have to struggle with it for long. She called me only recently and I came right down. We had the party she planned and then this terrible murder."

"A party!" Rob was pacing. "You're all crazy. Why didn't you refuse?"

"I couldn't. She was my friend. You know that; since we were children. She had made up her mind. All she asked was that I hold her hand so she wouldn't lose her nerve."

Lucy was sobbing. Sydney stroked her hair. "I'm sorry luv."

"Any more shocks?" Rob stared from Hale to Sydney, his eyes burning.

Hale shook his head.

"A question. How is my mother's body to be disposed of? It will probably be bizarre."

"She is being cremated. Following her wishes. The ashes are to be buried in a little cemetery in Italy."

"One more ridiculous expense."

"Rob you really are a jerk. Who cares what it costs if that's what Ma wanted."

"How are we to get the ashes there?"

"Sydney and I are to take them."

"Which means we can't get this thing really settled until after you make that little pleasure trip because I'm pretty sure that's included in the commitments."

Hale nodded. "I think we can work it all out."

"This is not the end. I bet the police don't know about the extra million. That makes you a prime suspect. Come on Lucy. Let's go." Rob started over to Hale and faced him across the desk. "I suppose we can still use the guest house until after the funeral even though it now belongs to you."

"Of course."

"I'm not coming Rob. Not just yet."

"Suit yourself." Without another word he rushed out.

Lucy stood up. "Poor Rob. He's so angry. And so greedy. I should have called Dad but Rob said he would. All they ever talk about is money. I wonder if they talked about Ma in a real way after she was dead."

"I asked Maude earlier, when she was talking of suicide, if she would like me to call Bob but she said one of you would."

"Thanks though." Lucy took Sydney's hand and helped her from the chair as she reached for Hale's hand. "Look guys, let's go to La Jolla de Mismaloya for a drink. The last light on the water is so pretty. Ma would like us to do that. Then we'll decide what else to do."

Hale looked at Sydney.

"Let's," she said, and still holding Lucy's hand, started for the door.

After Mismaloya there was El Set because that was where Maude took visitors to sit above the ocean and drink margaritas. News of the murder had reached Daiquiri Dicks. Dinner was on the house.

"Ma liked this place because the food's terrific and the service is great and she could just stroll down the beach for a couple of blocks, watch a spectacular sunset and feel right at home. Isn't it beautiful? I know I'm being sentimental but I don't want to go home yet and face Rob and the dark and think about Ma until time for the funeral at that awful hour."

"We're glad to be with you luv," Sydney assured her. "I'm feeling sentimental and sad too."

"Why don't we go to the Krystal and see what's happening at Bogart's?" Hale suggested. "That's your favorite spot Lucy."

Hours later, while they were waiting for Eloisa to open the door, Lucy sighed. "Well, now I have to face Rob."

"Then don't," Sydney said quickly. "I'm staying in your mother's room and the guest room is empty. Why don't you sleep there?"

"Gladly. Good night dear friends."

Hale kissed Sydney on the cheek. "Thanks for all your help."

She smiled as she hugged him.

"I'll drive over later and we can walk to the restaurant. It's already morning. We should be there shortly after six don't you think?"

"Yes, I agree. See you too soon," she waved as she crossed the patio.

Sydney was feeling lightheaded. It was almost two o'clock. She sat down to take off her shoes. The bed shuddered and then there was a cold nose on the back of her neck, followed by a sneeze.

She patted Corn and fell back on the bed.

"Go to sleep. You might as well stay for what's left of the night. I can't believe I'm taking you home."

In seconds they were both asleep.

"Lucy is just getting up. She said don't wait. She'll come along with Rob."

"You're certainly wide-eyed for one who considers noon early for an appointment," Hale observed.

"Actually I'm sleepwalking, but remember I was an actress and this is my early morning role when it is absolutely imperative. Panchita has made coffee. Would you like a cup?"

"No thanks. I'll wait until we get to the restaurant."

"Corn thinks it's too early for a walk," Sydney commented. His lead dangled limply as the three descended the steps. "I hesitated about bringing him but it didn't seem fair to leave him when everyone else in the house is coming to this last little get-together."

"Is he missing Maude?"

"I can't tell. She was away so often that he may just take it as a routine absence. He wanted to sleep on the bed. He loves to do that any time it's allowed."

Hale picked up the lead Corn was dragging. "We must make sure everyone signs the guest book or they won't get their bonus."

"That ten thousand dollar reward, as it were, still seems a little ludicrous."

"Maude thought it was a hoot. She described how different people would react. She said if Rob were not so young and strong he'd have a stroke when he heard it. You saw, he almost did."

"I thought he was going to explode at one point. Poor Rob."

"Don't feel too sorry for the poor spoiled little rich boy. I think Lucy was right when she called him a prick. Anyhow, Maude said Julia would cry when she opens the letter and then divide the money among her kids. Valenciana will laugh and use it to somehow benefit her business and Edwina will ponder a long time deciding how to spend hers and then probably give it to an animal cause or buy a fancy dog."

"Interesting, to any of the three of them it's not a whole lot of money but when a gift like that is unexpected there seems to be a responsibility connected with spending it."

"How will you spend yours?"

"Maude probably predicted I'd do something extravagant like buy loads of new jewelry. Or, perhaps she anticipated I'd pay off some I have already."

"You're exactly right."

"I haven't thought about it. Right now money seems unimportant. Alfonso is driving Panchita and Eloisa over. Afterward he's taking Lucy and Rob to the plane. Rob insists he has to get back immediately. They don't even seem curious about their mother's murder. I tried to persuade Lucy to stay but she thinks she should go with him."

"I told her last night that I'd like her to go through her mother's jewelry and anything else she likes. I forgot to mention, before Rob left in such a huff, that I am to dispose of Maude's personal things."

"Don't fret. You gave him a copy of the will and you know he has pored over it."

"I'm sure you're right. Lucy may come back later. I hope you'll look through the jewelry too. After Lucy goes over it I'll send you anything you fancy," he added.

"Our taste in jewelry was not the same. She thought I was far too conservative. But I must admit there are a couple of pieces I covet. At any rate, I hope everyone from the house comes but I'm not sure. Miguel is going to bring his mother if she is well enough. With her arthritis you never know. I don't know about Filemon and Reyes. I invited them but they both seemed a little uncomfortable about such a formal setting and all of Maude's friends who greet them in passing if they're working in the garden but probably don't even know their names."

They crossed Insurgentes, which was not yet busy, and descended the steps toward Le Bistro. "Unusual to be walking around in the dark at this hour unless I'm going home from some all-night occasion."

"What time is it?" Hale asked, looking at his watch. "Barely six-thirty. There's Doctor Rodriguez. You haven't met him yet. He was wonderful to Maude."

Hale introduced them and Sydney sensed gentleness and warmth immediately. It was no wonder Maude relied upon him.

"Let me take the dog and get him settled."

Corn wagged his tail as the lead went to another familiar hand. He trotted after the doctor out onto the deck.

Doctor Rodriguez returned carrying the collar and lead. "I'll leave these right here on the bar. He's not going anywhere so long as there is a party and a chance for bites. I came early hoping the coffee would be ready."

"I'm sure it is. I'll join you," Sydney said as she turned to a waiter. "Thank you for being so helpful to Maude. She mentioned you with such affection and I've heard from her friends how caring you were."

"It was a pleasure to care for Maude and to be her friend. A pleasure." His voice cracked. "I'm not the only early bird. Others are arriving."

After quick cups of coffee and lame jokes about a little early for drinks, several trays filled with glasses of champagne and Bloody Marys were emptied.

In the greeting line, Rob managed to be near Lucy and Hale while appearing to have his back turned to Hale even though he was standing beside him. Lucy was happy to see everyone and they hugged her with a mixture of laughter and tears.

Panchita and Eloisa stood near Alfonso, a little stiffly. Alfonso, as usual wearing a dark suit and a tie, was more at ease. Panchita had taken off her apron and had on a dark blue crepe dress she saved for holy days. Eloisa was pleased with the black and white mini-skirt her boyfriend had brought from Guadalajara.

Sydney went over to them. "Please join me. Over here." She guided them to a spot beside the river. "This was Señora Maude's favorite table. What would you like Adrian to bring you?"

Panchita smiled conspiratorially to Sydney. "Orange juice *especial*."

Sydney returned the smile. "Sounds perfect. I'll have that too."

Eloisa opted for champagne without hesitation. Alfonso decided he would have just a small glass even though he was driving to the airport shortly.

Julia, Valenciana and Edwina arrived together as expected. They looked over at the table they always shared with Maude. Sydney was amused when she saw a frown darken Valenciana's brow as Hale guided the threesome to a table beside the piano. But he sat with them and soon they were all enjoying champagne. Many of the guests stopped to pay their respects as if the women were part of the family. In their minds, they were.

Doctor Rodriguez, after his fourth glass of champagne, moved into the middle of the group and motioned for silence.

"One little Maude story," he began.

Sydney rose quickly but graciously from her table still holding her glass. As she linked her arm through his she said, "I'm sorry Doctor. Maude was definite years ago. No scripture. No hymns. No speeches. We'd all like to recall Maude escapades. I know I would. But those were strict orders."

He smiled agreeably. "All right. We must obey orders. I propose a toast." He lifted his glass high. "To our Maude."

Everyone stood. "To our Maude!" they shouted in unison.

Sydney lifted her glass. "To Maude," she whispered as tears ran down her cheeks.

"Sorry, I was carried away for a moment." Doctor Rodriguez, arms still linked, walked back to the table with Sydney. After greeting Alfonso and Panchita and Eloisa he sat down.

"Forty at last count," Hale leaned over and whispered to Sydney as he reached their table. "And Maude said fifteen max would turn up at this early hour."

"I'm not surprised. Please excuse me for a moment," Sydney said as she went over to Lucy and Rob.

"You've been standing here long enough and you've greeted everyone. Come and sit with Julia and Edwina and Valenciana and have a bite."

"Those old women don't interest me," Rob said sharply. "I never did understand what Ma saw in them."

"Rob you're awful. They were Ma's best friends down here and it won't hurt you to be nice to them for a few minutes."

"How long before we can leave?"

"About half an hour."

"I'm going for a walk."

"Come on Sydney." Lucy walked ahead of her to the table. "May we join you?"

"Of course," Julia welcomed them.

"I'm ready for champagne," Lucy said.

"I think I'll switch to champagne too. And I'm ready for food."

The others decided it was time for refills.

Lucy and Sydney were just finishing breakfast when Rob returned.

"I wish you'd eat something."

"I'm not hungry."

"I'll walk out with you," Sydney offered.

Lucy hugged her mother's friends and Rob nodded.

"Alfonso is waiting to drive you to the airport."

"In *your* car?"

"To you it is just an old car. You like it only because of its value. To me it is a treasure. I shall love driving it and I promise to take good care of it. And, don't forget I'm taking the dog off your hands," she couldn't help adding.

He winced the smallest smile and shook his head. "I could never decide if you were real. Even as a kid. It was exciting to have you come visit. You were beautiful and glamorous and you brought expensive, imaginative gifts and then you'd disappear."

Sydney placed her hands behind his neck and drew his head against her cheek. "Sometimes I'm not quite sure I'm real either Rob. But my love for your mother was."

"I know that and I should be thanking you. But I'm still sad and mad. I feel Ma was betraying us by planning to commit suicide. And you were helping her. I'm disappointed she left so much to other people. Even you."

"Come on Rob," Lucy called from street level. She had insisted that Alfonso put the top down and she was eager for a breezy ride to the airport.

"Love you," she called, and waved to Sydney as they moved away.

"Oh, it feels good to stretch out and be ready for sleep at a decent hour. I'm reading Madame de la Barca's *Life in Mexico*. It's charming but it won't keep me awake long tonight."

Corn appeared to be listening as he wagged his tail. Sydney laughed. "You don't care what I'm saying or what I'm reading." She patted the foot of the bed. "Oh, come on. Sleep right there."

Was it hours later? Or only minutes? Sydney was so deep in sleep that she couldn't be sure. She thought she had heard Corn bark. Just a little woof. She could barely see him standing on the foot of the bed, wagging his tail. As she reached for the light switch a gloved hand grabbed her arm and forced her back.

She screamed but another hand instantly covered her mouth.

She flailed her arms and legs furiously and managed to escape the hand. She screamed again. The bed shook as the man struck the headboard. Corn grabbed his shoulder, growling and pawing.

The intruder pushed Sydney aside and turned on the dog, knocking him to the floor. In long quick steps he was through the door, slamming it in Corn's face.

In moments the door flung open as Sydney found the light switch and slumped onto the edge of the bed. Panchita and Alfonso rushed into the room.

"What happened Señora?"

"I don't know exactly. A man was here. I tried to turn on the light. He knocked me back on the bed. We struggled. Corn grabbed him." She looked around. "Jesus. I thought he hit the headboard with his fist. But look. He sunk a knife in there.

"Call the police Alfonso. Don't touch the door knob. He was wearing gloves, I think, but don't touch anything."

Corn made a leap for the bed.

"No," Sydney ordered. "Stay."

He stopped inches from the knife.

Sydney reached for a pillow to cover the weapon and feathers spilled out. She gasped. There was a long slash. Her hands were shaking as she put down the mutilated pillow.

"That was close," she murmured as Panchita handed her a robe.

Shortly, a policeman knocked and immediately came into the bedroom. More prompt than Santa Fe, Sydney thought. He introduced himself in precise English.

"Can you identify the person?"

"No. It was dark. He was wearing black, or dark, clothes. A leather jacket. I could feel that. And leather gloves."

"Are you certain it was a man?"

"Yes."

"How can you be certain if you could not see?"

"I'm a strong woman and I was struggling for my life and I couldn't break his grip. The hand over my mouth was too big for a woman's. It was definitely a man."

"But you did break his grip. You managed to get free."

"The dog grabbed his shoulder and arm. He was growling and chewing, and clawing with his paws."

"There should be blood. Have you touched anything?"

"No. Except the pillow. I thought he had hit the headboard with his fist and then I noticed the knife. I started to cover it with a pillow so the dog wouldn't lick it and I saw that the pillow had been slashed. That is how close he came to my head." She hesitated. "I'm not sure you'll find blood. If I'm right about a leather jacket, Corn's teeth may not have gone through to flesh. The man ran after the dog turned on him."

The policeman removed the knife and placed the pillow in a bag. "I will leave an officer here for the rest of the night. In the morning I will return. Perhaps you will remember something more."

"What time is it?" Sydney asked Panchita as the police left.

"A little before three o'clock."

"I'm disoriented. When I heard Corn bark I was so sound asleep I thought I might be dreaming. Did you hear him barking?"

"No Señora. I heard you scream and I ran for Alfonso. Would you like it for me to stay?"

"No, thank you, Panchita. I'll be all right. But I am going to leave the light on," she added. Sydney then settled against the fresh pillows Panchita brought and wondered if she could concentrate enough to read. At that instant a figure appeared in the doorway. "Hale, what are you doing here?"

"Alfonso called and told me what happened. He thought you could use a little company."

"The police were here. They questioned me, and Panchita and Alfonso. Someone lunged at me with a knife. A big knife. He plunged it right into the headboard. It just missed us. Hale, I think that man was someone Corn knew. He just woofed. He knew that person."

"You think he knew who it was?"

"Yes. I didn't realize it at the moment. I didn't tell the police. But when you came in, just now, he gave a little bark and wagged his tail. He reacted the same way."

"Do you think it was me?" He chuckled but it had a slightly hollow ring.

"Of course not. But it was someone he recognized. After the man grabbed me and pinned me down and I screamed, Corn went for him but it was almost as if he had been surprised by what happened. It took him a moment to react. Panchita said she didn't hear him bark. She just heard me scream."

"Interesting. Now I'm taking charge. I'm going to get a big glass of Scotch for you. One for myself too. And I'm going to stay right here."

"We'll be glad to have you stay."

"Back with drinks in a minute."

In no time Hale was handing her a glass, straightening the bedspread, propping up a pillow and settling himself against the carved headboard beside her. Corn jumped onto the bed, licked Sydney's hand and flopped down between them with his head on Hale's thigh.

Instantly Sydney turned to Hale. "The light has gone on. Now I know. You and Maude! I'm glad."

"How did you figure that?"

"Corn is obviously accustomed to your being in this bed. How long?"

"Casually over the years. Lots of fun. These last few months there hasn't been a whole lot of what Maude always called 'rollin' around in the hay.' It's been a special time for me. I think for both of us."

"I'm sure. How have the children taken it?"

"Rob has never admitted it though I'm sure he knows. You could see how he resents me. And not just over the will. He had tried to get Maude to find another lawyer."

"Why?"

"He said my investment experience was not extensive enough. Actually I think because he knew Maude relied on me for advice in all areas.

"Lucy doesn't mind. When she comes here she likes to hit all the bars in the big hotels. You'd think being a bartender that would be a busman's holiday for her but she thrives on bar ambience. Maude didn't much like bars except the ones in her favorite restaurants. So, Lucy and I made most of the popular spots. One night we had been dancing at the Krystal and she leaned across the table and smiled in that intimate way she has and said, 'Hale, you're adorable. If it weren't for hurting Ma I'd be sleeping with you myself.'

"I must have reddened because she went on, 'Don't be embarrassed. I'm glad. Just don't ever do anything bad to Ma.' I assured her I wouldn't. About that time the band began to play and we were back on the floor and that was the end of it."

"I can understand Maude being attracted to you and I'm pleased for you both." Three days ago this man on the bed was a stranger, and now. "You are adorable Hale."

"So are you, Sydney." He grinned wickedly. "Shall we?"

"Hale, that's tempting but inappropriate under the circumstances."

"You're right. I'm sorry. You've finished your drink. Here, let me take your glass. You need to rest. Corn and I will sit here until you fall asleep. There are police in the courtyard. You're safe now."

"Sydney? Florian Gibson."

"Thanks for returning my call. I'm Tad Brennan's cousin. You remember we talked some time ago after you saved Kim's life. You called when I was in hospital in London after my. . . ." Sydney hesitated. "My accident."

"Shit, I remember. Tad let his daughter visit you and you got yourself, and her, involved with an ugly little green man in Ireland and got yourself pitched off a balcony. Don't tell me you're involved in something like that again."

"I need your help. In Mexico. In Puerto Vallarta. I came down here to help a friend commit suicide"

Gibson laughed. "Christ, who do you think you are, Dr. Kevorkian?"

"My friend didn't commit suicide. Before she could do that she was murdered."

Florian whistled. "Murdered! What do you want to do, solve this on your own?"

"I have to go home for a few days on business and I want you to watch after a dog."

"A dog! What the hell? You don't make any more sense now than Kim did when she was trying to tell me about the little green man disappearing. Does being vague and confusing run in the family?"

It was Sydney's turn to laugh. "Probably when we're stressed we do ramble on. I think the dog knows who the murderer is so he may be in danger. Please. Come tomorrow. I'll explain everything when you get here."

"I'm not keen on Mexico. They're not keen on black guys down there. I've been there only once a long time ago and it was a disaster. I nearly got myself killed."

"I believe that's when Tad saved your life," Sydney said slowly.

"Sydney Reardon you don't play fair. Yes, that's when your cousin saved me. Five hundred dollars a day and expenses. O.K.?"

"Fine."

"I'll be there tomorrow."

"Let me know what time you arrive. Alfonso will meet you."

"Think he'll recognize me in the crowd?"

"I think so," Sydney replied easily. "And I think I'm going to like you Florian Gibson."

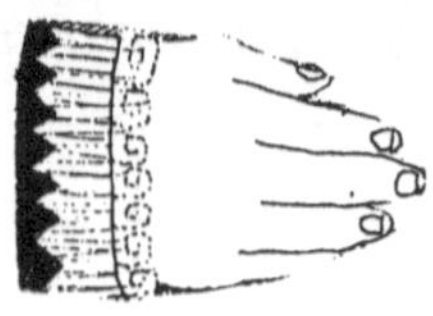

"Hi big boy."

Corn sat on his haunches and tilted his head to gaze up the full length of the tall man. After a pause he decided upon a tentative wag of his tail.

Florian Gibson knelt on one knee. He flattened a huge hand on the portal floor and gave three quick pats. "Come on. We'd better get acquainted. You're going to be answering to me for a few days."

Corn hesitated, his usually curled tail at half mast.

"Come on."

One step. The dog stopped and surveyed every inch of the patio as if there were many interesting and unusual sights he'd never noticed before.

"O.K. old buddy." Gibson turned away and moved to the edge of the pool where Sydney was standing, watching with amusement. "He'll come around."

She nodded.

"I'd like to meet everyone who works here or who has access to the house. And I'd like to talk about who's in the will. Who are her friends?" He grinned. "Shit, I know I'm here to watch a dog but I'll be thinking about the murder too. I'd like to help."

"Florian," Sydney began, "I don't know."

He held up a hand. "If you don't want me snooping just say so. Won't cost you anything extra," he added.

"It's not that I don't want you snooping. The police have gone over and over the questions. And I've gone over and over them and I'm nowhere."

"It's not your business."

"I thought we'd have dinner in. You can enjoy one of Panchita's marvelous meals and, if you wish, you may ask questions. It will be simple to gather the staff before dinner. Alfonso took your bag to the guest room. Would you like to rest for a bit while I get everyone together?"

"No. I think I'll take a walk on the beach. I want to see them one at a time, not in a group."

Sydney quickly executed a mock salute. "Yes sir."

He looked at his watch. "What time do you want me back here?"

"In an hour or so."

"I'll be here."

"Right through there if you want to go to your room. Onto the next portal, first door on the left."

Florian closed the wrought iron gate as Corn started to follow. The dog stood looking through the bars, whimpering. He waved to Sydney and, ignoring Corn, walked away.

"What would you like to drink?" Sydney asked as Gibson returned to find her seated on a handsome straight-backed colonial bench in the formal salon.

"Gin."

"A martini?"

"No. Just over some ice."

"Alfonso will get it for you."

He had not noticed Alfonso standing at the far end of the long room.

"Would you like to begin with Alfonso? I know you talked as he drove you in from the airport but you may have more questions."

"Sure."

"Shall I leave?"

"No. No. Stay. You may notice something I don't. I'm not going to really question them. I just want to get acquainted and observe. Christ, I'm not here on official business. Just to watch a dog." He laughed. "Where is he?"

"On the portal. I thought he'd be a distraction. Look. His nose is pressed against the grill. Now that you've ignored him he can't wait to make friends."

"Your drink sir."

"Thanks Alfonso. Mrs. Reardon and I were just talking about that great car. You must like to drive it. And take care of it." He shook his head. "A big responsibility though. Do you use the same mechanic all the time?"

"I do almost all of the work myself," Alfonso answered with pride. "If it is major there is a specialist who comes from Guadalajara."

Sydney sat quietly admiring Gibson's friendly casual approach. The conversation was over in five minutes. When Alfonso left the room Sydney walked over to Florian's chair. He was jotting notes on a folded piece of paper.

"I'm impressed," she said, when he stopped writing and looked up. "You don't seem to be asking questions at all and after those few minutes you know where Alfonso was born, how long he'd worked here, what he did before, his age, where his mother lives, his favorite bar in town, that he likes to fish, when his wife died, where his children are." She paused for breath. "Amazing."

"Very good. And, that he's going to put away his inheritance from Señora Maude and let it earn interest for his old age which he is going to spend in Morelia where he grew up. Fun isn't it," he added lightheartedly.

Panchita smiled her pixie smile and before the interview was over she knew that Florian Gibson liked steak really rare, didn't care much for chicken, could take shrimp or leave it, was lukewarm about spinach and never in his life had eaten all the chocolate cake he wanted at one sitting.

Filemon, the gardener, was off for the day to go to Sayulita to see his daughter and her new baby.

"I'm leaving quite early but I've left word with Panchita to have Filemon talk with you," Sydney explained.

Reyes, who helped Filemon, was surly and seemed to resent the conversation, not just the questions. Possibly because he was embarrassed that Alfonso had to translate for him. He alone had refused to go to class to learn English and Maude had let him stay because he was so clever with plants and willing to do heavy chores.

Eloisa was frightened and fascinated by the friendly black stranger asking questions. She giggled more than talked.

Miguel didn't want to talk about his military days and was silent and sullen when Gibson asked why he didn't finish his tour of duty. He was startled by the question, not realizing he had revealed that information.

"Must I answer?" He turned uncomfortably to Sydney.

"No. Forget it. Easy enough to find out," Florian said before Sydney could speak, and went on asking about the days when his mother worked for Señora Maude.

Sydney had expected Florian to continue to talk about the staff when they sat down to dinner but he just commented on the beautiful dining room, took a sip of his drink, and smiling, cut into Panchita's appropriately rare steak.

"Maude would look at that and say, 'I've seen a cow get hurt worse than that and get well.' Maude used more clichés than anyone I've ever known."

Florian laughed. "Just the way I like it."

"Interesting," Sydney mused. "When Maude used trite sayings they were appropriate, not just old and tired."

"I wish I'd known her."

"I wish you had too. You'd have liked one another."

"I'm getting to know her through you and the others. Why was she so hell-bent on killing herself?"

"Her heart had gone bad. I don't know the details. She didn't explain much in medical terms and I didn't pry. She faced being an invalid in a short while and she knew she couldn't live like that. I understood. If you had known Maude you would have understood too. Just keeping her alive was not a favor. Her only hope would have been a transplant."

"How old was she?"

"Not quite fifty."

"Shit. What a bummer. Who stands to gain the most from her estate?"

"After the children, Hale Howard, her lawyer. He gets the house and a sizable amount of cash."

"What about Alfonso?"

"He wouldn't. He couldn't. He was devoted to Maude. Besides, both Hale and Alfonso knew she was planning to kill herself so there would have been no need for either of them to murder her."

"And you knew so you're not a suspect."

"I should hope not."

"Everybody is a suspect. *Everybody*. You've told me there was such a mob in the street that anyone could have stabbed her and gone unnoticed."

"That's true. Almost everyone who'd been at the party was there. But there were also thousands who weren't at the party." Sydney paused thoughtfully. "Florian there's something troubling me."

"Oh?"

"I noticed a knife on the floor of the car, almost hidden under the front seat. It was similar to the one lodged in the headboard. But why Alfonso?"

"I told you. Don't assume innocence. But don't assume guilt either. Thanks for telling me. What about friends?"

"Her closest were Edwina Mead, Valenciana Tello and Julia Lundgren I think. Julia is almost eighty. A taxi was waiting for her and went off through the mob immediately. She wasn't on the street when Maude was stabbed. Edwina would probably faint at the thought of blood, much less the sight. Valenciana might have the courage and the strength but I'm sure she doesn't know anything about knives."

"There you are assuming again. Do you know who Ellen and William Craft were?"

"No."

"No reason you should. My mamma told me about them when I was little. She said we were distant relations. I never have known if that was true or if she just wanted to give me a little pride and push.

"They were slaves who escaped from Georgia in the late 1840's. That's not too unusual. Others escaped too. It's how they did it.

"Ellen was light-skinned enough that she could pass. She was going to travel as a frail young white man and William as her servant. She put on a man's suit and hat and boots and a big overcoat. They knew someone might notice her smooth beardless skin so they muffled her face in a scarf and said she was suffering from a toothache. She couldn't read or write but they solved that by putting her arm in a sling so she wouldn't have to sign hotel registers. There was another problem—Ellen's high voice. William must have been a quick thinker because he told her she'd be deaf and dumb so she wouldn't need to speak.

"It worked. They finally made it to Boston where they told their story and became celebrities. The news traveled back to Georgia and after the Fugitive Slave Act of 1850 was passed their owners sent slave catchers after them. Just in time they fled to London where they stayed until after the War."

"What a great story."

"Isn't it. I used to have Mamma tell it over and over. She always stressed don't assume, you can't take anything at face value, and if there's a will, there's a way." Suddenly Florian laughed. "I guess Mamma used clichés just like Maude."

They soon finished dinner and moved onto the portal for coffee. The afterglow of a perfect sunset cast pink streaks on the mountains at the far end of the bay.

"Back to the lawyer."

"Hale. He's young, bright, handsome. He had Maude's complete confidence. He's short. You'll have to bend almost double to look him in the eye. She left him an astonishing amount of money. And this house."

"They were fucking."

"You certainly put the relationship in perspective quickly," Sydney said with surprise. "A romantic description of their relationship too, I must say." She laughed. "How do you know?"

"The way you described him. I don't give a shit how tall he is or if he's handsome. That's the way women describe a man when they're having sex. You and him too?" He grinned. "I'm kidding."

Sydney could feel herself blushing. "No, but it crossed my mind."

"Must be a horny bastard."

Sydney laughed again. "There's something else I should tell you." She paused.

"I know."

"You know what I'm going to tell you?"

"No. I know there is something else."

"How?"

"You stood up and walked along the porch while we were talking. You turned around and came back but then you walked away again. You've been straightforward about everyone else but I knew you were holding something back. What?"

"Jesus, you are frightening. Do you always zero in like this?"

"Always," he said firmly but his eyes twinkled. "Go on."

"I'm certain Hale is innocent but he does have a motive." She hesitated. "I feel I'm betraying a confidence."

"Did he say you couldn't tell?"

"No, but I'm sure he didn't expect me to discuss it. Though, for all I know, he told the police."

"But you don't think he did."

"No. Maude had a life insurance policy worth several million dollars. It had a provision that added an extra million if she was killed in some accident. Or, if she was murdered. That million she left to Hale."

Gibson whistled. "I'd say he sure as hell did have a motive. Could he have stabbed her?"

"No. He had gone on ahead to try to get Alfonso to bring the car closer. He. . . ." Sydney stopped. "Wait. He came back. He was frustrated because he couldn't get the car through the crowd. He wanted to make sure she was all right. He stood close to her and tried to tell her, above all the noise, that they'd get the car through somehow."

"How do you know that's what he told her?"

"That's what he said when we were going over it later."

"Could he have stabbed her?"

"I don't think he could have. I certainly don't think he would have."

"You don't want to think so. Visualize the scene. Was it possible?"

"I suppose anything was possible in that mob but I don't believe Hale is guilty. Why don't you let me set up a lunch date? Get to know him and see what you think."

"Fine."

*H*ale Howard stood on the porch at the entrance to Café des Artistes and watched the black giant walk easily up the steep cobbled street from the waterfront.

"You must be Florian Gibson," Hale said as the man took the steps two at a time. He held out his hand.

"How did you happen to recognize me?" Gibson grinned.

"I don't know. Maybe the size. Sydney said you were big. Or the color." He returned the grin. "Glad you're here. Where's Corn? I thought you weren't to let him out of your sight."

"Alfonso is taking him for a ride. I didn't know if he would be welcome here."

"Oh, he would but I'm sure he'd rather go for a ride."

They were standing in the big open bar facing the *trompe l'oeil* wall of sky and clouds and an expanse of perfectly appointed tables.

"Fancy place."

"Isn't it great? The food is great too but I chose it because of the murder. What will you have to drink?"

"Gin."

"With?"

"Ice."

"Come here for a minute." He led Gibson along a narrow walkway above street level and pointed halfway down the block. "Right there."

"Sydney said there was a mob in the street."

"More people than you can imagine. If you were moving with the crowd you were just pushed along without any choice. It was almost impossible to move against the flow.

"I looked down and saw that the police car was behind Maude's car rather than clearing the way as we had planned. I was so irritated that I left Maude and Sydney by themselves while I tried to get the car in closer."

"So you were down with the car when Maude was stabbed. Not anywhere near the actual scene?"

"Yes. No. I fought my way back to make sure Maude was all right and to explain the car situation. I must have just started back to the car when Maude was killed." He turned away from the porch rail and looked up at Gibson. "You knew that didn't you?"

Florian nodded.

"Come on. There's nothing more to see out here. Let's have lunch. In the garden. That's my favorite spot."

After they were seated Hale picked up a menu and then put it down. "If you're a steak man I recommend the beef."

"I'm a steak man."

"Good. Then let me order for us."

"You and Maude were fucking," Florian said abruptly when the waiter left.

"It's pretty hard to embarrass me but that comment makes me uncomfortable."

"Not trying to. Just want you to know what I know and hope you'll tell me what you know."

"Surely Sydney didn't tell you that."

"I figured it out."

"I won't ask you how. I loved Maude. You didn't know her and you don't know me. With the age difference you might question my sincerity but I assure you it was for real."

Gibson sipped his drink and remained silent.

"Sydney told you about the insurance policy didn't she?"

Gibson nodded in agreement.

"I suppose plenty of people would say I had a motive. I'm already getting three million and the house. You could call it absurd greed if I'd kill someone I loved for another million."

"I'm not a good judge. I've spent thirty years talking to guys who'd stab you for a pair of Nikes."

"As Maude would point out, you do, by god, call a spade a shovel. I've told the police about the insurance."

"Good."

"And I told the children. Rob was furious. Said I hadn't heard the last of it. Lopez-Gomez, Maude's representative in Mexico City, is competent so I expect we have heard the end of it."

"Have any ideas about who killed Maude?"

"I don't. I've gone over it a dozen times. I can't imagine Maude having any enemies. Now I have a question for you. Are you really here to watch a dog? I'll bet Sydney called you to come down and solve the murder."

"You're wrong. Christ, I can't believe it either, but I'm really here to watch a dog."

"Why?"

"Because Sydney asked me."

"Must be a pretty strong tie. Want to explain?"

"Why not? Years ago, many years, Sydney's cousin saved my life. I was a rookie cop and I volunteered to go way down almost to the Guatemala line and bring back this jerk who'd finally been trapped for drugs and half a dozen other crimes of across-the-border importance. I thought it would help my career.

"I'd no more than stepped off the damn plane when I got zapped in an alley. I'd have died right there if Sydney's cousin hadn't dragged me out and up to his hotel room. He's a doctor. He was on his honeymoon. He and his bride nursed me until I was strong enough to go home."

Gibson grinned. "Didn't do a whole hell of a lot for my career. But if anyone in that family calls I come on the double."

"This is Edwina Mead. We hope you will join us for lunch at Le Bistro," the slightly overly-enthusiastic voice on the line was saying.

"Us?" Florian Gibson asked noncommittally.

"Julia Lundgren, Valenciana Tello and me. I suppose we are—were—Maude's closest friends here in PV. We're lost without her but by going to our favorite places we almost feel like she'll walk in. Oh, and bring Corn. Baby's coming."

"Baby?"

"My Great Dane. She and Corn are good friends and they like to be out."

"Thank you. What time?"

"Around two."

Florian felt uncomfortable. Everything was too perfect. His companions were a study in expensive pastels; the clear shallow water flowed over the river rocks with just enough vigor to be heard; and the fellow back there who played the white piano made listening easy.

Corn sighed and stretched full length on the deck lulled by the music and the sound of the stream. The Great Dane was already asleep.

The three handsome women were excessively pleasant. Florian smiled and lifted his glass in response to their *Salud* and wondered if any of them had ever been to lunch with a black man.

They had invited him to join them. Now let them tell him why. He smoothed the white square that covered the blue-grey tablecloth and waited.

"We heard Sydney has gone back to the States. We hear that you were an important law officer in New York and are here to investigate Maude's murder," Julia began, taking the lead because she was the oldest. She shook her head nervously and took a sip of her margarita. Florian liked her.

Before he had time to answer Edwina added, "We've heard that Maude left a lot of money and the house to Hale and the children are upset. We were all surprised by that bizarre funeral, if that's what you'd call it." She giggled. "But of course we were all pleasantly surprised by the ten thousand dollars." Gibson had yet to decide if he liked her.

"I should think the police here could solve the murder quite efficiently. We are somewhat puzzled by your presence as an investigator." Florian was pretty sure how he felt about Valenciana. And how she felt about him.

He placed his elbows on the table and leaned forward in a guardedly friendly manner. "Ladies you have heard too much and assumed more than is the case. I am here to watch a dog."

"A dog?" they exclaimed in unison as if rehearsing the line for the Greek chorus in a college play.

"A dog." Florian Gibson grinned slowly as he enjoyed their surprise. "You must have listened to speculation. But you don't seem to know that Maude left Corn to Sydney Reardon. She had to return to Santa Fe for a few days. She called me in New York and asked if I could come down and look after him. She believes he can identify the murderer so he may be in danger. Sydney's cousin saved my life years ago so I couldn't refuse. As Señora Tello has so rightly observed, the police here can solve the murder quite efficiently."

It was not what they expected to hear but they asked no more questions and ignored him charmingly as they chatted about clothes, parties, luncheons and salon appointments.

They recommended the shrimp stuffed with ham and cheese. He enjoyed it. Maybe he did like shrimp after all.

He was not sure he believed the white ladies as they took their leave saying they hoped to see him again.

"Shit," he muttered to Corn as they climbed the few steps to Insurgentes.

"Want to take a walk old buddy? I think you're bored." Florian Gibson shook the dog's ruff playfully. "I don't have to say walk twice do I?"

Corn was dancing ahead of him in the hall around the Talavera bowl where he knew they kept his lead. Florian settled the soft leather collar around his neck. "Thanks," he said as Eloisa opened the wide front door. "Back in a little while."

Lights twinkled around the bay. The few strollers on the beach paid little attention to the big black man and the big black dog on the paved walk that separated the hotels from the sand.

"Wish I could let you run but I don't think that's a good idea." A couple of local curs circled, challenging Corn. He stared them down and trotted on with his stiff-legged Chow gait. Florian trotted behind him enjoying the warm tropical evening.

He didn't see the figure standing in the shadow on the wall beside the path until it was too late. He felt the steel in the flesh of his shoulder and loosened his grip on the dog's lead for an instant as he groaned and staggered. The man had a head start but Gibson was strong and fast and he was closing the distance, ignoring the blood running down his arm. In seconds the two men and the dog were splashing through the water where the lagoon of the Rio Cuale emptied into the bay.

The assassin was headed for the rocks that jutted out into the water from the end of the sea wall. "Get him," Florian shouted. "Get him Corn."

With a lightning burst of speed the dog caught the man's foot as he scrambled up the rocks. An arm swung and a clenched fist drove a knife blade through Corn's forepaw. He yelped with pain but chewed wildly at the moving legs above him. There was a scream as teeth sank into an ankle. The struggling, shadowy figure flailed with the knife trying to cut through the thick ruff to the dog's throat.

"Hold on Corn."

With his good left hand Florian grabbed the leg above him on the rocks. He jerked the man down onto the beach and as the knife came up Florian kicked it away and jammed his foot on the outstretched wrist. He stepped back. "Get up. Get up you motherfucker."

Florian Gibson gasped. "Miguel!"

Corn growled low in his throat.

"Easy boy." He looked at the blood dripping from Corn's paw. "Move." He reached for Miguel's uninjured wrist. "Don't even think about running you little fart or I'll kill you."

A couple, walking along the beach just visible under the lights at the edge of the sand, stopped to embrace.

"Help!" Florian said in a loud voice. "Police."

They looked around. He didn't know whether they heard him or not but they moved on quickly and were lost in the darkness.

Miguel was sobbing, and limping from the gash in his ankle where Corn's teeth had reached the bone. His broken wrist dangled uselessly. Gibson pushed him back through the shallow stream. Corn hobbled along dragging his wet lead. They almost stumbled over a figure lying on the beach.

"You speak English?" Florian asked as he prodded the sleeping bag with his shoe.

"Yeah," the kid answered, yawning.

"Get up. Go for help. Police. Ambulance."

The boy looked up at the huge man and was immediately on his feet running toward the lights of a hotel.

The three were struggling slowly up the street when the ambulance and police car arrived.

"What the hell?" Gibson said indignantly when the officer indicated they were going to the police station rather than to the hospital. "The dog could bleed to death. We could too," he added.

The young cop lifted his shoulders indifferently and nodded in agreement. "Maybe."

"He tried to kill me," Miguel wailed.

"Should have killed the son-of-a-bitch."

"Maybe. We go now." The policeman lifted Corn into the ambulance and motioned the men in after him.

Gibson was irritated. The cop had latched onto "maybe" the way foreigners often repeated a favorite word. What the hell. He used his good hand to pull himself into the vehicle.

The officer behind the desk raised an eyebrow in response to Gibson's request for a call to his lawyer.

"You have a lawyer? Here in Vallarta?"

"Yeah. Don't try to lean on me buddy. I can teach you how it's done. I want to call Hale Howard. Now."

"Señor Hale?"

"Now."

The policeman behind the desk hesitated.

"Maybe," the officer who'd brought them in said. "He has Señora Maude's dog and he's bleeding."

"I can see he's bleeding."

"No. The dog is bleeding."

The desk officer looked up Hale's number, dialed and handed the telephone to Florian.

"I'm at the police station. Need your help right away.

"Meet me at the police station," Hale said after Eloisa had brought Florian to the telephone. "I think you know where it is."

"Funny," Gibson replied dryly. "What's up?"

"Miguel has confessed."

"It's about time.

*

"Tell me in English," the round police commandant instructed Miguel. "Tell me in English so Mr. Howard and Mr. Gibson can understand."

*

"Sit here. Please." The officer indicated chairs on each side of his. "The boy has told me everything. He will repeat it for you. Begin."

"I, I, I believe. . . ." Miguel's jaw was shaking. "I believe she was a witch," he mumbled.

"Speak up."

"She was a witch," he muttered, barely audible.

"A witch! Maude?" Hale Howard leaned forward in his chair. "That's ludicrous."

"Please Mr. Howard. Just listen. We will talk when he has finished."

"Sorry."

"Continue."

"My mother," he sobbed. "My sister," he went on so rapidly, crying and mumbling, so it was almost impossible to follow him.

"He thinks Señora Maude caused his mother to have arthritis so she cannot work. And that she pushed his sister so she fell and broke her leg and it is not right so she cannot walk as she once could."

"The dog," Miguel blubbered. "The black dog." His voice was stronger. He raised the cast around the wrist Florian had broken and shook it in defiance. "The black dog tried to kill me." He turned eyes bright with fear and hate toward Florian. "The black man tried to kill me."

"Should have killed the little fucker," Gibson muttered.

"Mr. Gibson!"

Hale nodded to Florian.

Miguel gained confidence. "Now Señora Sydney will have the black dog. She will be a witch. I will kill her!"

"I think you have heard enough." The commandant motioned the guard to take Miguel away. "I am concerned for the safety of Señora Reardon," he said as soon as the prisoner was out of the room.

"I take it you're not going to let this guy out and he'll eventually be convicted. He killed a prominent foreigner. He's admitted it. And Sydney will return from the States and be here for at least a couple of days."

"These people—how do you say it—superstitious. They believe in witches, some good ones, some bad. They believe in *chupacabras*—goat-suckers, vampires, blood-sucking bats. And they believe black dogs can bring bad luck. He had never seen a black dog with a black tongue before. Miguel thinks it can belong only to a witch. He is now something of a hero. He has killed a witch. There is much talk. There will be another who will need to kill a witch. It is best that the señora not stay. When she is gone and the dog is gone perhaps we can forget witches for a while." The policeman shrugged. "Or perhaps they will find another witch."

The commandant shook hands with Hale and raised a hand in farewell to Florian as he opened the door for them.

"Will you keep an eye on Sydney until she and Corn can get out of town?" Hale asked as soon as they were alone in the hall. "You know Alfonso is going to drive them all the way to Santa Fe."

"Sure. I don't think there's much danger. The policeman may be superstitious too. He wants the whole thing over with. I hope he's not spooked enough to let the little bastard get out."

"I'll watch for that. I take Maude's murder personally. I'm going to see to it that he doesn't get away with it."

On the steps of the station Hale looked at his watch. "It's almost noon.

I'll buy you a drink. And lunch."

They walked in silence for half a block and then Hale chuckled. "I'm a softie. That kid was blubbering away about witches and I knew he really believed in that kind of evil and for a second I felt sorry for him. Then I thought, he killed Maude in cold blood. And he tried to kill Sydney. He almost killed you. That sympathy didn't last long."

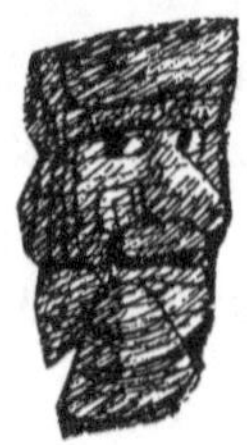

"I told you we wound the Maypole. Here." Sydney was dressed but had slipped off her sandals and was seated, propped against pillows on Maude's bed, a photo album open on her lap.

"You two were pretty cute," Hale observed. "I see Panchita gave you your favorite breakfast. May I have that last bite of brioche?"

"Of course. She'll be happy to fix breakfast for you if you'd like."

"No thanks. I had coffee."

"Look. Here is the house Maude and Bob had in San Gimignano. And there's the cemetery she wanted to be buried in."

"I hate to interrupt this stroll down memory lane but you need to be on your way. You have a long drive. There aren't many four-star restaurants between here and Mazatlan. I've brought paté and that Chihuahua cheese you like, fresh *bolillos* and fruit. There are three bottles of good wine and Panchita has fried chicken. Alfonso and I have packed the car and Corn is pacing in the patio wondering what is going on."

"Thank you dear heart."

"Come." He took her hand and helped her off the bed.

As she put on her sandals, she turned to Hale. "I know I'm putting off leaving. It is the end of an era and I'm reluctant to let it slip away."

"I know. And I'm sorry to see you go. But you must. I have to say you look great in jeans. I wouldn't have imagined you wearing them but they're great."

"I don't now own any but I'm going to buy a pair when I get home. Lucy left these. They're a bit short but so comfortable. Should be good for the drive."

"I wish you'd let Alfonso take the car and Corn to Santa Fe and you fly home."

"That would be sensible. But I'm probably going to be as protective about that dog as Maude. I have to be certain he gets home safely. Besides, I've always wanted to drive over the Sierra Madres from Mazatlan to Durango. Almost every guide book describes the route as the most spectacular in Mexico. And, before we head up that long barren stretch to the border, we're going to backtrack to Zacatecas. I've been wanting to go there for years."

"Taking the dog home is turning into quite a trip."

Corn bounded across the courtyard to greet Sydney and Hale, ignoring his injured paw.

"Ready?" Florian picked up the dog's leash and started toward the patio door. "I don't like the idea of you and Alfonso driving after dark."

"You don't believe those tales about tourists being hijacked," Sydney said lightly.

"No I don't but shit, it could happen." The lead tightened as Corn planted his feet. Florian turned. "Hey, old buddy, come on."

But the Corn Dog did not move.

Florian shortened the lead. As he moved closer Corn growled and bared his teeth. Gibson jerked lightly on his collar. The dog shook his ruff and backed up, pulling the lead. Another jerk but the dog stood his ground.

"Let me try Señor Gibson." Alfonso took the leather strap. "Corn, *perro*, come." He inched forward, holding the tether taut. Alfonso took a step and Corn pulled back and growled.

"What's going on?" Hale asked.

"I do not know Señor Hale. He is growling and will not move to the door."

"He's upset," Sydney said. "I think he realizes something has happened to Maude."

Almost without seeming to move, Florian was on his knees stroking the dog's back. After a time he encircled Corn with his long left arm and used his fingers to caress his head. The dog stiffened as he was lifted but, reassured, gave his captor a quick lick as he was taken out of the patio and placed on the back seat of the car.

"I'm distressed about leaving you with so many loose ends Hale. I can stay a few days more if I can be of help."

"No. Go now. I want you out of town and safely on your way."

Sydney hugged Hale and turned to Florian. "Thank you for coming when I called."

"You're welcome but Mexico is not for me. Thirty years ago I almost got killed down here and now I come back to look after a dog and get myself stabbed." He laughed.

Sydney reached up and put her arms around his neck. "Come to Santa Fe to visit Corn and me. It's friendly there, I promise."

The two men waved as Alfonso eased the Cadillac over the rough cobbles.

"I'd better see about getting out of here and you better see about getting on with your life, white boy."

Hale grabbed his companion's arm. "Let's follow them for a ways. I'm concerned and the drive through the jungle to Tepic is pretty interesting. There's an O.K. place to have lunch and then we'll turn around and come back."

Hale quickly led the way to a shiny white Jeep parked on the street. "IT'S A JEEP THING" Florian recited as they approached the vehicle. "What's this sign on the back window about?"

Hale grinned. "Just what it says. If you're not a Jeep guy you don't follow. Maude gave me the four-wheel-drive for my birthday last summer and the decal with it. Neat. I like it." He backed around. "We'll give them a head start. Alfonso won't drive fast. He loves that car too much. It will be easy to keep them in sight. There they are," he pointed as they headed north.

"That's the marina over there," Hale said, becoming the tourist guide. "And that's supposed to be a replica of one of Columbus' ships. It was brought here after the five-hundredth anniversary celebration. You can go for a cruise out on the bay and have dinner. They shoot off fireworks along the shore. Maude rented it for a party when it first sailed in. I wasn't around but they tell me it was a great bash."

"Are you going to stay on now that Maude's gone?"

"I think so. I've got that great house. And plenty of money. If I get bored I can build up a practice."

"Shit. I bet in three years you'll have gone native."

"You may be right. Want to stay here and go with me?"

"What about Alfonso and Panchita and the rest?"

"I'll keep them on."

Florian was looking in the side mirror as they talked. "A new black Mustang convertible has been following us since we left town. Slow down and see if it passes."

Hale eased up and the car sped past but then slowed.

"Stay behind it for a while."

The Mustang braked slightly.

"Pass it."

They tried to see the passengers as they drew alongside but the windows were tinted.

"Couldn't see a thing."

"No," Florian agreed as he watched the mirror. "Now here it comes again." The car zipped by. "I don't like it. Could be hijackers. Or drugs. Who the fuck knows. I don't like it at all." He reached under his loose-fitting polo shirt and pulled a gun from the waistband of his pants.

"You have a gun!"

"Yeah. I thought it might be a good idea after all that's gone on. I bought it here."

"You bought a gun here?"

"Easy. Here or anywhere. No fuss and not too much money. You can buy one anywhere in the world. When I leave I leave the gun. Want it?"

"No. No, I don't want it."

"No problem. I can find somebody who does."

"Is that what they call a Saturday Night Special?"

"Right. Easy to buy and sell. And to use. Pass that car, and cut them off."

"What do you think I am, a stunt driver? How do I do that?"

"Just pass and get far enough ahead to give them time to stop and straddle the road. Then we get out fast on the far side."

"And if they don't stop?"

Gibson smirked. "Then we made a bad call."

"Too late. They're playing the game. Passed us again."

"Janey, slow up. Stop! They've blocked the road."

She slammed on the brakes and the sleek car came to a halt at the edge of the pavement a few yards from the Jeep. "Don't open the door. Let's see what they do."

"Look. They're getting out on the other side."

"There's a gun!"

"Where?"

"Right by the windshield."

"You're imagining things."

"They hollered something. Look, you can see the gun now."

"It's a Negra."

"Sweet Jesus Martha Sue, you sound like you got out of Mississippi in the sixties instead of the nineties."

"I don't know. I. . . ."

"They're telling us to get out of the car with our hands up."

Janey opened the door slowly and stepped out giving a tug to the bottom of her bikini before raising her arms above her head.

She tossed golden curls and smiled. "Don't shoot," she called out as she took a step forward. "I'm Janey. That's Martha Sue." She looked around and motioned. "Come on." Her voice lowered. "I'll take the black one. I like him. He's big and old and tough. I bet he's plenty good. You can have the little white one. Come on," she repeated.

The other woman eased languidly out of the car. In one hand she held the top to a bathing suit. She waved with the other. "Hey there."

"Hijackers? Drugs? I do believe we've been attacked by a pair of Southern belles," Hale drawled. "I'd better move out of the middle of the highway before we get broadsided by an eighteen-wheeler."

"Take your time. I can handle this."

"Yeah Mister Big Time Cop. Be careful. You never can tell," Hale laughed.

"We saw you two guys as you left town and thought you might want to have some fun. We were just playing. You scared us when we saw the gun."

"You could get yourselves killed or raped or robbed," Florian was saying as Hale came over.

"We might have killed you in self-defense," Hale explained. "We thought you were hijackers or drug runners." He grinned. "Who the fuck knows?"

Florian threw a finger Hale's way and turned to the young women. "There are plenty of crumbs down here who'd kill for that fancy car."

Janey moved closer. "Go on. You're cute when you're stern like that."

Gibson shrugged and shook his head. "I give up."

"We couldn't see a thing with those black windows. My friend is right. You could get in big trouble. What are two pretty girls doing riding around by themselves?"

"These two aren't any fun," Martha Sue concluded as she draped the bra around her neck and started for the Mustang.

"Don't be so hasty," Janey advised. "We're models. We just did a commercial for a hotel in Vallarta and we're doing one for the same chain in Mazatlan in a couple of days. We decided to drive. The car's rented," she added. "Want to go to Mazatlan with us?"

"No, I don't think so."

She turned to the big man. "You don't sound like a Southerner." She stopped abruptly and blushed.

"He's a cop from New York," Hale explained.

"Ooh, how absolutely exciting," Janey purred as she sidled closer to Florian.

Suddenly they turned at the sound of a short beep from the passing automobile.

"Gorgeous old convertible," Janey remarked. "Much rather have it than this little thing."

The men stared as the Cadillac disappeared around a curve, a hand still waving from the passenger side.

"That lady knows you."

"She certainly does," Hale admitted.

"She your girlfriend? Or your mother? Your daughter?" Martha Sue grinned.

"None of the above," Hale said. "But we are traveling with them.

"Shit. How did we get ahead of them? We have to be going. You girls be careful."

"You two looked like bad little boys caught smoking on the school ground," Sydney said as she jumped out of the car laughing. "The two of you standing there in the jungle talking to Thelma and Louise was one of the funniest sights I've ever seen."

"It wasn't that funny," Hale protested in embarrassment.

"Oh yes it was."

"You know them?" Alfonso was puzzled. "They are Thelma and Louise?"

"No, we don't know them. We just met. They're actually Janey and Martha Sue. Sydney is just teasing us." Hale was still red but smiling.

"We can explain," Florian assured Sydney.

"I'd rather write my own script. Dialogue isn't necessary. Just watching was a riot."

"They are models on the way to Mazatlan."

"And they wanted you to go along."

"Something like that. It must have been pretty funny to see us there." Florian chuckled. "How did we get ahead of you?"

"I heard a noise and stopped to look at a tire."

"You roared by and when we saw you we knew why."

"The girls were so pretty and not wearing clothes." Alfonso began to grin.

"They were wearing clothes." Hale was defensive. Then he laughed. "But not many," he conceded.

"Why are you here?" Sydney asked, becoming serious.

"We wanted to be sure you got out of town safely," Florian explained. After the threats and the witch talk."

"We did quite well getting out of town," Sydney teased. "I'm not sure how safe you two were."

"We were going to follow you to Tepic and have lunch there and go on back."

"We can have an early lunch here with all the goodies," Sydney invited.

"No," Florian said emphatically before Hale could respond. "We'd better get back and you should put a few more miles down before you stop for lunch."

Sydney started to protest but thought better of it.

"I have something for you Alfonso." Gibson reached under his shirt. "It might come in handy. You never know."

"I don't like guns," Sydney shuddered. "I certainly don't like having one in the car."

"If you would not be upset Señora Sydney, I would like it."

"Do you know how to use a gun Alfonso?"

"Yes, Señora."

"It's yours." Gibson handed it over. "If I were you I'd toss it before you cross the border."

Once again the two men stood waving as the long car pulled away.

"Do you think it was smart to give Alfonso the gun?"

"Who knows? I hope he never has to use it."

"You turned down Sydney's invitation. In fact you were abrupt."

"We've gone far enough."

"Shouldn't we follow them at least to Tepic as we planned?"

"As *you* planned. You're a whole lot too concerned."

Hale reddened.

"Let her go old buddy. You're too clean-cut to have been doing it with Maude and then switch right over to her best friend."

Hale laughed as they stepped into the vehicle. "You've been thinking about Sydney too."

"That's putting it delicately. But she's way too classy for me. If you can understand a Jeep thing you ought to understand other basics. Turn around."

www.ingramcontent.com/pod-product-compliance
Lightning Source LLC
LaVergne TN
LVHW051015080826
845145LV00009B/2640

* 9 7 8 1 6 3 2 9 3 1 0 8 5 *